WITH AND WITHOUT CLASS

WITH AND WITHOUT CLASS

BY
DAVID WALLACE FLEMING

"An Anniversary Concession"

—*Out of the Gutter:*
The Hard Times Issue, Spring 2008;

"Perfection of the Mind"

—*Escape Velocity, the Anthology, March 2011*

SHORT STORIES

Fantasy | Science Fiction | Horror

AN ANNIVERSARY CONCESSION

"YOU DON'T GOT cop hands," Ryan said, "You got hands for playing the piano."

Eric considered his thin fingers. "Are you getting out of the car?"

"When did you first decide to be a cop?" Ryan asked.

"It doesn't seem like I thought..."

"You're being sensitive, again," Ryan said. It was dusk. His full, acne scarred cheeks were backlit by a distant streetlight as he smirked. "Thanks for covering the rest of our shift, rookie." He pointed to the dispatch radio, "Just listen to this. Do what it tells you." He looked around with a playfully conspiratorial air, "Now, Eric, if you have to shoot somebody,"—his small eyes twinkled—"it's draw, point and squeeze. Don't do any of that snapping and jerking I seen you doing on the target range."

"Alright, Ryan, but please," Eric said, "Make sure you return the favor next week—you know I—"

"Pop the trunk then, bitch." Ryan got out. He carried a duffle bag around the cruiser. The guy was nuts for bowling.

I'm ready, Eric thought. *Just remember. Remember all those fucking dispatch codes.*

Ryan slammed the trunk, then slammed the passenger door with his ball bag. He had stuffed his button-down navy shirt into his duffle but, as a six-three guy in an undershirt and polyester pants, he still looked a lot like a cop ducking out of the last few hours of his shift.

Eric drove from the curb and continued on Forty-Second. He could hear Charlene's slightly nagging voice, see her wagging her finger at him. *Aren't you serious about us? How could you forget to take off work for the first anniversary of our wedding?* He would never admit to anyone, least of all Ryan, but he knew he absolutely couldn't let Charlene know he'd forgotten their anniversary. He had to make dinner reservations, be home early with flowers, the whole thing. He was proud of himself, in a way, for fixing his mistake like this. He just had to coast through two more hours on a Tuesday and then Ryan would owe him, and would cover for him next week.

He turned left on Carriage. Streetlights lit cracks of a vacant firehouse's brown concealment coat. Between shadows, fresh blue paint shimmered with the tag NO HOPE!

The radio issued: "Dispatch to Eight-Tango-Twenty, over."

Eric stared at the radio, then he unlatched the black-corded transmitter, "This is Eight-Tango-Twenty, over."

"Code Three. Investigate a three-seventeen at the Thirty-Second and L Smart Mart, over."

Damn. Eric pulled to the curb. *Thirty-Second and L...* "Eight-Tango-Twenty to dispatch, that's affirmative—"

He looked to the empty seat.

"—we're on our way, over."

His siren bleeped as he flipped the switch and pulled a U-turn. He pressed the gas. The brake lights of a grey Datsun glowed red. Eric swerved around the car. It shrunk in his rearview. His tires squealed as he turned right on Thirty-Eighth. *You'll call for a supporting unit—but that doesn't make sense.* He pressed the gas. Cars parted in front of his gleaming black hood. *You'll just go. You can handle this. Nine times out of ten it's nothing, anyway. You know that. Just take care of this and Ryan will owe you big.*

He pulled into the Smart Mart's lot. It was dark. The yellow, backlit banner sign flickered and hummed above big windows. A lone fill-up hose had been left splayed across the grimy cement beneath the gas canopy. His heart hit against his ribs as he parked by the tire inflation hose, away from the glass front.

He opened the glass door. The store's dusty, outdated merchandise was lit to a white gleam with buzzing fluorescents and muzak hummed softly. *What's that smell, what's that smell? Hotdogs and... sulfur? ...gunpowder?* No one was sitting at the beige Formica booths along the windows or walking near the freezers. His right hand rested on his holstered Beretta. His other hand felt empty. *What's wrong with you?* Eric looked behind the checkout counter, between shelves of WD-40 and Christmas tree car deodorizers. The black register till lay empty on the tiles.

He drew the Beretta. *Nothing. Maybe—*

A shuffle of footsteps—his stomach fell faster than gravity—his mouth dried. From between rows of shelves, a lanky man in a brown T-shirt and tattered navy tuxedo pants shoved a short woman. The man had a creased, taxed face like a used-up rock star.

Eric winced and stepped backward. He drew and aimed between the man's eyes.

Buzzing fluorescent lights lit her face. The thin, creased skin around her eyes revealed the outline of her cheekbones and her short Notre Dame shorts showed-off her tan, toned legs.

The man clutched her straight red hair near the base of her skull and rammed a shotgun against her neck. He repositioned the barrel, exposing a tennis-ball-sized bruise on the inside of his needle-tracked forearm. Rose rings flushed around his eyes and his marble-sized pupils quivered.

A rubber band fought one side of the woman's braces and she muttered *"please"* over and over, soft and fast.

Eric yelled, "Drop—!"

The man's eyes shattered. "I don't have to explain—"

his feminine voice wheezed, "You can't see the beginning—can't see the end—only what's here!"

She cried, *"Please!"*

Eric's hands squeezed to align his red dot sights beneath the man's temple. He blinked to stop the dots from bouncing. It didn't work. *Can he see my hands?* The Beretta's rubber grip slickened. *Don't let him leave. Take a shot if it's clean.*

She trailed a "please" with a gasp.

"Drop the gun, NOW!"

The woman moaned.

The man said, "Listen to me," he walked her toward the entrance.

Eric stepped back. He cocked. "STOP! Don't move!"

"NO!" And then he mumbled, "Listen. I'm hold'n it," his nostrils flared, "I'M CHANG'N! And fix'n and walk'n... talk'n."

"STOP!"

The man's eyes begged: "Listen. LISTEN!"

A drawled "please" escaped from the woman's rubber band latched braces one more time.

Eric tried to steady his aim on the man's temple. *Clean. Clean. Clean. Steady. Clean.* His sights bounced.

Eric's heel struck a raised tile edge. It couldn't have been any thicker than a quarter. His Beretta exploded. Bits of the cartilage of the man's ear scattered behind and he staggered, pulling the barrel backward. Her neck mushroomed crimson, propelling geysers, speckling warm across Eric's face. Buckshot riddled a plastic cigarette sign by the checkout counter and her grimaced face turned upside-down as her head rolled off to her side. The head bounced against the tiles with a crack before her body fell.

The man's hand slapped to his ear, "NOBODY!" He thrashed his head, "NOBODY! NOBODY! NOBODY!"

The Beretta exploded three more times. Red mist flashed over the man's face. He fell onto a shelf, popping and crumpling plastic Doritos and Tostados beneath him as his shotgun clamored and slid.

"Jesus! Shit... God." The Beretta fell. The handle clinked. His hands searched his chest and stomach for wounds.

The buckshot had hit the cigarette sign.

He collapsed onto the checkout counter and used his arms for support. Then he twisted toward the glass doors and his numb legs followed. The glass door swung silently closed behind him, sealing off the brightly lit store from him with its hot guns and the girl's lifeless head. Eric staggered on past his police cruiser toward the dim yellow streetlights.

THE HEAT

THE AHEARA'S HULL groaned and folded. It burst up with licking flames as we escaped in the lifeboat with my thumb dead-stopping the outboard's throttle. I clutched the flare gun in my other hand. The Aheara's bow upturned, sinking in a vortex of the midnight Pacific.

Part of the pulsing redness that ringed the research vessel broke off and followed us. It skimmed waves, closing the gap.

"Majaar!" I screamed through the wind and the waves. He huddled and shook in the bouncing bow and clutched his fifth of whisky. "Majaar!"

He didn't answer.

"Everything cool, Samples?" he asked in some distracted malaise. He shivered with that fishy skin respiring near his horned cheeks. He was losing it. But I was still just Samples to him—still just the human technician.

"I feel sick," Majaar said. "My memory's blurry."

"Part of it broke free," I said. "It's following us."

"It needs heat. It must be some form of virulent wasteform."

"What?" I yelled. "That's what this is? Our plastic and your—Veronian-bio-engineering?"

"SK5,"—the lifeboat crested and Majaar clenched the side lip—"I told the chairman we had to monitor the Veronian and the terrestrial waste streams sooner."

"SK5?" I yelled.

Old memories surfaced.

"SK5," I mumbled. "The building blocks of your smart plastics? But,"—I aimed the outboard motor away from a breaker—"SK5 is harmless as long as it's deactivated before it's released"

The pulsing mass skimmed and broke out behind us, revving like an engine.

Majaar shivered. He cowered in the boat and drank. "On normal scales, sure. On mass scales—here in the Pacific's gyre with the native plastics… We—we knew this would happen. I told the chairman. It's not my fault." He looked over my shoulder at the approaching mass. "It goes haywire when it coalesces at mass scales."

"This happened before."

I remembered all the knowing looks I'd seen. Not just *Dimension Jumpers*—humans also.

"It gets hungry. It turns on us. But we're so dependent on the technology. We just find new worlds."

"You colonized other worlds and had your garbage use the native plastics like—like shapeless hermit crabs."

"A thousand times," he admitted. "We're so smart." He took a drink. "We never learn a thing."

"How many strains of the fluid-based AIs do you think were floating out there in the gyre?" I asked.

"Hundreds—thousands." He closed his eyes tight. "We grew them all for backwards-compatibility. The syntho-neurons are viscous—you've seen the magnifications of how they flow over each other; right? for greater interconnectivity. The hotter it gets, the smarter it becomes. That thing's burning up from the heat of the Aheara's fire! We're both dead."

My heart pounded and my thumb was numb against the throttle with the ocean mist blinding me as I searched out the black horizon. The thing couldn't have been more than two hundred feet back there—

"I'm gonna be sick," Majaar said.

The red mass surfaced through black waves. It dimmed and sunk beneath.

I slid the satellite transponder across the hull to him. "Call in our position."

He stared at the transponder and looked dizzy for a moment.

The fuel gauge on the outboard was moving to red. "We didn't leave the ship with much fuel. We're running out of time. Call in our position." I stabbed toward the transponder.

He stared up at me, vomiting milky chunks over himself and the transponder. "Where are we? Where *are* we?"

The wind died. The outboard bucked and sputtered. We were slowing down. I looked back and let the throttle loose. "I—I lost it." I turned to him. "Majaar, it isn't behind us! I lost it. I can't hear it. Where is it?"

He pulled off his fifth with the vomit all over himself and looked distractedly out toward the distant, flaming Aheara. "Probably diving beneath us. Then it surfaces in a ring, trapping us like it did the Aheara."

"I don't know if anyone else had time to call in our position," I said. "Quick!"

Majaar stood. He picked up the transponder and scraped idiotically across it with the neck of his whisky bottle.

"What are you doing?" I asked. "Call in the position."

I rubbed my sore hand, unbreached the flare gun and loaded in one of the cartridges from my pocket.

He threw the transponder overboard. He looked over at me:

"What are you doing with that device?"

"It's a flare gun, Majaar." I trained it on him. "You know what a flare gun is, don't you?"

"How did you operate it?"

"You're becoming one of them; aren't you? You're forgetting the little things. Just like the captain before he drank... What's inside the bottle?"

"What happened to the device in your hand?" he asked. "I need to know. It's important for me."

"What's in the bottle, Majaar?

"That's how it spreads; isn't it? The alcohol keeps it sterile before it reaches the bloodstream. The captain drank from Nikolay's flask. Then they went nuts and torched the engine room.

"Why? Why torch the engine room? For the heat?"

"How did you change it?" Majaar asked. "That thing you hold—how did you change it. It's important you tell me."

"Pour out the bottle over the side."

He looked into me and smiled. "I'll pour it—"

"No. Wait."

He turned the fifth upside down. Grey slime oozed onto the floor with plopping sizzles. It flashed in specks before pulsing red. The thing hesitated and fanned out. Then it stopped and coalesced in a blob. It headed toward me.

"Stop, Majaar. Call it back."

He looked back up and laughed. "It's been growing inside me. I've watched it destroy so many times on so many different worlds. Now, it's inside *me* and I know what it feels like to be part of the burning redness. It feels like home."

"Stop it. Call it back!" I pressed into the aft lip of the lifeboat and thought about jumping overboard. The mass was below us now, waiting to encircle.

The glowing sludge scorched the steel beneath it in

a thin, black streak. It burned and slid with stuttering back and forth hesitations like a taunting dog.

"How many cartridges do you have for the device? How many does it take to activate it?"

"The device?" I asked. I held the flare gun overboard. "I'll drop it."

"No," Majaar said. "We need it. Give the heat. Be careful, Samples."

The glowing slug stopped, inches from my foot. Its throbbing glow warmed through my steel toed boots.

"That's why you followed me to the lifeboat—*the flare gun?*"

"The heat," he said. "Tells us more of the heat. Tell us: how hot is the device? How long will it keep us warm? How long will it keep us flexible—keep us pliant?"

"Forever," I blurted. "You'll be warm and flexible—you'll be pliant forever. I swear." I looked down. "Call it back!"

He made clicking noises and it moved toward him. It slid up his leg and over his chest, burning his clothes and charring his smoking flesh on its way. "Come home. Come home," he said and it turned grey and slipped into his mouth.

"Now," he edged forward, crouching low. "Give the device."

I looked at the flare gun, then at the distant, burning Aheara and the black horizon. "Okay." I pointed it at him.

"No. First—"

The flare imbedded into his chest and his ribs ballooned outward before the grey slime pulled him back together. It seeped out of his skin and his whole body gleamed a blinding red. "It's magical," he said, wobbling and struggling to stand. "Each sector I've visited—all the pleasures I've experienced. This is the center point, Samples. This is what I've always been waiting for and what I knew I deserved. It loves me."

The red ring rose out of the water. It revved and tightened around us.

He turned on me: "Now—you burn for heat."

I picked up an oar and jabbed him off balance and the oar caught fire.

He wobbled and looked over at the icy black waters.

I jabbed him again and the boat rocked.

"No," he said. "It's mine,"—he looked over at the icy waters—"*The heat wants to stay with me.*" He hunched himself lower in a defensive stance, preparing to lunge. "You can't hate me; can you, Samples? You can't hate the spark for wanting to live."

I jumped on the left lip of the hull just as a wave struck. The lifeboat capsized and I was sucked under into the cold blackness. As the waters swirled and shook me I managed to open my eyes long enough to see a flailing red ember sinking down. It sputtered out in a storm of steam geysers. I groped around and found the edge of the lifeboat and slowly pulled myself out flat over the top of the overturned hull. Up above, the rescue copters lit up the waters and the lifeboat. The red slime oozed up the boat, burning my leg and my clothes. It was a slow burn. It was tired. The size of its catch had been overestimated.

It shared so many secrets—secrets I didn't deserve: every love, every ambition, every shiny new product and toy—all heat. And the source of it all touched me, giving itself freely, unselfishly. "So warm," I muttered, "so warm—*so warm.*"

The liquid nitrogen cannons went off from the copter's decks. I felt it shiver and die. It asked why it had been betrayed after giving its love so freely.

I laughed and muttered, "All my desires: All heat."

A BLIND DATE FOR BONKERS

LOOKING THROUGH THE lens of his microscope, the first thing that came to his attention was that when these creatures, which he deemed considerably humanlike—when they talked, they didn't say things in the way you or I would say them. That is, one word after the next. It took him considerable time to decode their language. They exchanged by utilizing a singular outburst. All of their syllables and ideas were scrunched into this quick, sharp outburst so that whole sentences, whole ideas, whole narratives came out as isolated, singular sounds. Of all the sounds available, their unit of exchange sounded most like a bonk. Whenever these humanlike creatures conversed, they did not so much talk as bonk. To put it another way, they were Bonkers.

These bonking Bonkers bonked all night long. They bonked on cell phones, in trains, they bonked in burgundy, overburdened beds. They bonked in groups going up stairs and sometimes going down these stairs.

When they were angry with each other, they bonked each others brains out: bonk, bonk, bonk. They didn't even think before they bonked. They did it in excited, exuberant ways. And this was exciting to watch through the microscope. Sort of a peep show for people.

What would happen with these Bonkers from time-to-time is that both a male and a female would expend all romantic options and turn to outside parties to help form an alliance. This was called a Blind Date. It was called a Blind Date because neither party was able to see the other prior to their first meeting.

There was this one couple that got set up on such a date. The male was named Mason foot because he had this sedimentary thing not completely unlike a foot. The female was named Cola Eyes since her eyes beamed sugary, caffeinating brown.

Before Mason Foot left his abode for the evening, he bonked a trusted female friend: "How does my foot look this evening and since it is what helps me bear my name, does it bear it well?"

She bonked back: "Modest male friend—true companion, I have never lied to you and, so, as such, now I bonk: Might've you of done something to fasten up the chariots and guard the oarsmen against a foul wind?"

"What?" Mason Foot bonked in befuddlement. Bonking being a relatively new form of communication among Bonkers since Bonkers had evolved their entire civilization incredibly quickly—in a matter of weeks, actually.

"Oh, I don't know," she bonked. "It *is* masonry but *is* it also a foot? One can never be too sure. Do this: speak to her in high-pitched squeals and prance it about. But, be masculine. Be erudite; be calm; be poised; but be rugged and masculine. Be a lover and a fighter, be both poet and prince. Be modest as a pauper and kind as a saint. But, use trickery if it be to both your goodly advantage. If her back itches from intemperate, stray weeds, buy her a newspaper and read some funnies. If the funnies turn her aghast with melancholy, swear to her you understand her mythologies of mirth. If she eats a bite, nibble the feathery ostrich and find an usher that can seat you promptly for the show."

"Sound advice!" Mason Foot bonked. "I got my wordsworth—and twice!" he bonked again.

Later on, both Blind Date Bonkers were seated at a fancy restaurant that had flaming gobos and honey-sweet swatting shimshams with tintercating mismots. Neither of them had released a single bonk from fear and nervousness of being the first to bonk and, of course, also of over-bonking. Presently, the waiter appeared and bonked thus:

"Dear sir and dear madam, would you like to hear me bonk of these specials? This is not important. I have already bonked—ha ha! you cannot listen to this message in part, or can you?—ha ha! We got rice cakes, we got pandas, we got noodles, we got gurbbling, singsong mashed potatoes and things that go slurp beneath your soup. Please do not sloup your soup, we have a strict policy on that and we enforce it sometimes if we're bored or we're all spunty. If you wish to sloup your soup, fill out this flout and undress each other with ravenous complibents... We got shellfish, too."

"Just a couple of snot shots to start, please," Mason Foot bonked and the waiter left.

Still neither one had let out the first bonk of the evening. The tension splouted.

But then it happened. Both bonks flew out of their mouths at exactly the same time and hurtled through the air and crisscrossed the table and struck them at exactly the same time and they both sounded nearly like this:

"My—! you are pretty (or handsome) and I was nervous coming here but now I see that this *was* a good idea. I find you attractive but I don't want you to butter my toast with margarine on this, our first date (or, I wouldn't think of buttering your toast although it seems lovely and fresh) and even though it would be fun and who doesn't enjoy a little extra dairy. Is it hot in here? Have you ever driven to the moon on a moldy mattress? (a trifling narcotics reference popular that week) And could you please give me directions to your warm, buttery toast. Kidding. Just kidding. Not really kidding though."

The waiter returned promptly with their drinks and bonked: "And has the lady decided on the main mourse for the meavening?"

Cola Eyes bonked: "She has...but with size-nits. This here, yes this? Of course this, the first item transisted:

Can this sandfist be a maco? Can this aldedo sauce be magorgen and then be vaporblized to nothingness before it be brought? Can one of the most senior smooks in the kitchen guess me my blirthblay?"

"All this can be done and more. Would you like the coat rack to arrange for flaming gobos and swattering mismots to dance and sleer as you chew?"

Cola Eyes slimmened her cola eyes, "I sniz sarcasm in your bonk, waiter."

"Not at all, madam. Rest assured that I would never bonk sarcasm at you. I merely stepped on a sharp meable just before bonking and may have mis-bonked. It won't happen again. And for the gentleman?"

"Another round of snot shots, sneeze, and a big, pig squish-out, medium dare."

"Excellent choice, sir. I'll bonk this repeatedly at the kitchen."

Cola Eyes bonked: "Wow, Mason Foot! Two rounds of snot shots, a fancy restaurant *and* a big pig squish-out, medium dare, you really are fussing out all the flops this meavening. I'm squished inwards in permanent by your powerful pushouts. Wait? Do you have enough green-backs to pay for all this partying? Oh...I shouldn't of nibbled that inside this bonk. Regardless, I have not brought green-backs. With you being from a good family and coming so well recommended, I maglooned the male would meter the meal and practice the compulsory panty-praise. But, some femzots bonk panty-praise is being dosed in globs of gooey suffocating glue. Will you pay for the meal? Have you brought enough? Do you hold the art of panty-praise high above you, Mason Foot?"

His bonk expelled: "Panty-praise is held high by me. If an old woman wants to dross the geat, I sprowse her in zords of glop. If a young girl wears a pretty print dress, I spin her around in smirckles until she vumpkins. If a horse hobbles into a train station, I punch its gonads. All these actions are maintained by me. You see? Toast worthy! Opps—misbonk! Disregard mid and end bonk! Wait. Disregard entire bonk. I rebonk this one."

"Never mind your rebonk, Mason Foot. I simply want to know if you brought enough greenbacks. As you know, I arrived here later and did not get a chance to great you in the meeting room. How many salamanders have you beneath the table?"

Mason Foot picked out the small cage hidden beneath the tablecloth and presented it for her appraisal. "Two salamanders. Two salamanders with which to pay. You see? All is well. I have brought the necessary amphibians. Buttery toast—misbonk! Misbonk!"

"Two salamanders! That will be plenty. We could do quite a lot with two, whole salamanders!"

"I have trained them since I was a boy. Wake salamanders! Speak to the lady!"

A leftmost salamander scampered back and forth nervously in the cage and stood and adjusted his spectacles and bonked, "I don't trust this one, master. She will never show her toast. She will not serve you as well as us. Please master. What did we do wrong? How have we offended you that you should exchange us in such a risky endeavor? Other salamanders have been sacrificed before in this way and for what? They have not been treated well by the restauranteers. The female's bellies grow full—we toil, master. We toil! Don't be a fool! I know a nice female over on Slibberbing Jablibberbing Boulevard."

"Back underneath the table you go."

"Why have you trained your salamanders to bonk thus," she bonked.

"It is not I that bonks through them. They bonk for themselves."

"We must spend them then," she bonked. She looked angrily to her meft. "If money offends me, it *must* be spent."

"Don't trust her, master," the bonk rose and hung in the air.

Then the food arrived: the big pig squished out with spruzzles and glasses of poultry magornzo and snit glowing candles and fumbly snails sliding in mello and whole pine-rabbles popping over chimneyed candy-fickles with gimmie gummy goose gumps and with whirly fuzz-plaster all fussing about.

"Now this is a meal," Cola Eyes bonked.

"Agreed."

They forked it into their mouths and bonked and bonked more freely with each forkful. They bonked of weather and music and hobblysnort. They bonked of

Merly and Pearly and of the winds of the West. They bonked of how many times they'd buttered toast and how many loaves they'd sent back to the baker and under what conditions and the refreshing feeling of getting the bread out of the plastic. They bonked of mortgages and blorgages and variable credit-frosting arms and legs and tentacles. And at the tail end of this, with a mouth half full of gimmie gummy goose gumps, Cola Eyes let loose a slippery spontaneous bonk that went thus:

"It's important for me to trust the Bonkers that surround me. I'm not picky about everything but there are certain things that are important to me. Last Wednesday, I went to the mall and bought a shirt and a flirt and that reminded me of my brother which reminded me of my moothmush which reminded my of my many speckled list of things that are a must for me to have in a bonk-partner. The first of which being that he must have a handy chazz-whiz..." And the bonk went on like this. Mason Foot examined it in parts, never being able to know for sure exactly how long it would take him to digest and understand the entire bonk, but it seemed, as he analyzed it and turned it over in his mind that it might take him seven, whole weeks, at the very least. The scientists of their day had predicated that their entire civilization could only be sustained in the most optimistic of circumstances for about six and half more weeks. If he added his lifetime to the lifetime of any potential bonkers he might sire he couldn't see his own bonk-line lasting more than four more weeks at best. But he liked this girl and he wanted to understand her bonk. He got nervous and bonked rather bonkishly:

"Cherrywood nipples!" He bonked it loudly so that everyone in the restaurant could hear.

"What?" she bonked.

"Nothing."

"Did you just bonk, 'Cherrywood nipples'? What's that supposed to mean? That's like something a crazy Bonker would bonk. I mean, I've heard some crazy bonks in my day. Cherrywood nipples? Cherrywood nipples? Are you feeling alright, Mason Foot?"

"I'm fine. I'm fine. I just. I just got a little nervous."

"That's your response to my test bonk? The test bonk that I give all Bonkers to see if they just want to butter my toast. The one that should take a Bonker seven weeks to debonk. The one that was supposed to take you to the end of civilization to debonk. You debonked my test bonk in a couple minutes and then you come back at me with cherrywood nipples? What's that mean? That's so weird. I'm not sure how I feel about you now. I'm not comfortable with this. Cherrywood nipples? You're weird. I think I hate you, Mason Foot. What kind of name is that, anyways? I bet it's not even sedimentary."

"I don't just want to butter your toast, Cola Eyes."

"You want to be a weirdo dweebie-vent is what you want to do. Cherrywood nipples?" Then she really started bonking. She let out bonks that were even longer: eight weeks, nine weeks, yearlong, abysmally-mysterious hyperspace bonks, bonks from beyond the grave warning of future plagues and famines, bonks inter-stitched with entire transcripts from fable orators of old, bonks overlaid with ghostly bonks of pirates tempting him with buried treasures and secret, magical potions. It was too much. He wanted her bonking to stop. It had to stop. Somehow.

"Cherrywood nipples," he bonked again. And scooted his chair back. It had worked before.

"I'm using my cellphone to call for a ride to come pick me up," she bonked.

"You don't have to do that. I can magurgle you *all* the way home in my chariot."

She raised her suspicious cola eyes up from her cellphone to him. "You just want to butter my toast."

"Setting that issue aside. I *can* magurgle you all the way home in my chariot. It's no trouble, really. It's the vimbleblest thing in the Glack."

"Cherrywood nipples!" she bonked to herself disgustedly as she pecked at the keypad. "I've made my mind up!" She pecked the keypad and a small hairy arm popped out of the side of her cellphone. "No!" she scolded the cellphone and smushed the arm back into the side of the phone. She pecked at another button and another arm popped out of the other side, then a small wriggling foot, then another foot. "No!" she bonked. Long brown hairs sprizounted out all over the cellphone and it bit her on the hand before dropping to the tablecloth and scuzzywagging all over the meal, scimscabbling down along the tablecloth to the floor and scuttling across the carpet.

Cola Eyes put her head into her hands and flobbed.

Mason Foot broke his attention away from a Mootball game broadzooped on one of those gazillion salamander mirrormorks and bonked, "What's wrong?"

"My cellphone."

"Yeah. What about it?"

"It hamstered!"

"Didn't you get the insurance?"

"Yeah, but not against hamstering!" She flobbed in her hands.

"Oh…I only ask because my spunky uncle splurges on such precautions. It is no big deal. I have already told you that I will magurgle you all the way home in my chariot. It's no trouble, really."

"I already told you that I don't want to be magurgled in your chariot. I want to call for a ride." She flobbed. "Cherrywood nipples!"

"Stop bonking that! It was a misbonk!"

"There are no misbonks!" She flobbed. "You don't glove me!"

"Keep your bonks down! We're in public. I just met you! How can I know if I glove you? For Course Rakes, I just wanted to get my toast buttered. There, I bonked it. Are you bappy?"

She looked up at him with her smeary, bleary cola eyes. "At least you're being blohnest now."

Mason Foot sighed. "Let's get up and go find you your hamster phone."

The hamster phone had crawled up onto the table of an old fatherly and matronly couple having their anniversary dinner and it was wrestling with whatever was slurping beneath the female's soup.

"May we please retrieve my friend's hamster phone from beneath your slurping soup madam?" Mason Foot bonked.

"You may," the madam bonked impatiently.

"There's no use," the passing waiter bonked. "Any fool knows that the only way to transform a hamster back into a cellphone is for both blind bonkers to agree on a wish for the hamster to grant."

"I wish for a bonker who tries valiantly to debonk my test bonks."

Mason Foot set his salamander cage on the table. "And I wish for a cheap date that lets me butter her toast." "Ditto bonk!" The salamander grasped the bars of his cage, nervously. "One wish," the waiter bonked, waging his finger.

"Then...then I wish that we both have a pleasant evening," Mason Foot bonked.

"Yes...I agree." And Cola Eyes beamed upon Mason Foot kindly.

The hamster phone burst up out of the soup, grasping desperately at its rim and gasping for breath. "Impossible wish! Impossible wish! Warranty voided! All insurance claims rescinded!" it bonked frantically just before it was pulled back beneath the soup by whatever was slurping below.

Just then the skylights above the restaurant flooded with blinding yellow light and a broad structure with pink ridges descended above the sky which was above the skylights. The broad, ridged pink structure rose and fell against the sky making the whole restaurant and the ground rumble and shake. "HEY THERE LITTLE BUDDIES! WHAT'S NEW TODAY?" an incomprehensible voice boomed from above.

Mason Foot flattened into a flat pancake shape with his hands flapping out near the edges of the disk and his stubby useless feet below just allowing him to wobble and worble his disk toward the exit door as everyone else was doing except the salamanders who clung together tightly. "YEAP! YEAP! YEAP!" Mason Foot bonked up to the broad pink structure in the sky as he warbled with the rest toward the door. "YEAP! YEAP! YEAP!" they all bonked upward toward the sky.

The incomprehensible voice boomed, "THE DUST MICROPHONES KEEP SAYING THEY'RE 'YEAPING' AT ME? WHY DO THEY ALWAYS DO THAT?"

ZOMBIE CLOWN WESTERN

THERE WERE SEVEN of them left—eyes bloodshot, worn thin. They waited for the sun to spill over the emptied saloon of the dust blown town. Montgomery and Tallboy had pulled a bunch together—mostly drifters—shiftless types. None of the bona fide men could be convinced to stay behind.

"It's daybreak that brings 'em," Montgomery said from his usurped position behind the bar. He slapped his Schofield down and held a locket to the lamplight, admiring a grainy photo. "Not sure why it's each year on this singular day. Faces painted all over—*stone-dead flesh*. Not a body knows where they come from. Not a body knows how they get painted gleam-like in that morning sun: Whites. Reds. Yellas. All colored. Them teeth—"

Tallboy's glass clinked and rolled over the floor. "I ain't afeared a no clown!" He stared off.

Montgomery slapped out a whisky bottle. "Take

another, Tallboy. Just to steady that hand—get these dealings behind us."

"You heard it?" Tallboy stammered. "I ain't afeared."

He patted Tallboy's trembling hand. "I heard."

Franklin got up and braced his Spencer rifle behind his broad shoulders to stretch and look out to the stirring doors. "Been in plenty scrapes. Figure it don't come to much who takes offense to who. All I need to know is: how much me and my boys stand to collect?"

"There's a payment coming," Montgomery said.

"I says: how much, old man? We ain't staying up all night—spinning yarns—talking ghost legends a marauding painted-face ghouls for our betterment. Me and mine, we came up north outta Kansas City and Cheyenne. We's known men. We been all over these parts. We been to Big Whiskey, Horse Hoof Whiskey... Ahh...? Lemme see: Whiskey Whiskey Whiskey. We know how things work 'round here in these upper-middle territories. We know there's fools running loose in these towns. Fabricating stretchers. Wasting a feller's time. We ain't got patience for treachery."

"Fifty dollars cash!" Montgomery said. "I told it before. That's my word."

"A body?" Soup Spoon asked from the corner of the room.

"A body," Montgomery nodded agreement.

Footsteps creaked over the boardwalk outside. Tallboy stopped drinking. "It's just—just near daybreak, I reckon."

Horse Sense and Post Notch shimmied their chairs and set their hands on their pistols.

The doors stirred.

White Lip and Post Notch drew, squinting into the dim light.

"Ledbrush!" Montgomery cried at the figure standing in the threshold. "Ledbrush what you doing here?"

He stomped out a thin cigar under his boot. "Howdy boys. Thought I'd find some fools held up in this saloon."

"You almost got shot's what ya did."

The tall man looked over the men. "Ya'll look like smart men... mostly." He pointed to Montgomery and Tallboy. "What these fools told ya? Told ya there's dead clowns a-comin'; did they?"

"That's what they's saying, mister," Franklin said. He slit his eyes and took a step toward him and looked around. "We's just about had enough, I s'pose."

"As elucidated prior, name's Ledbrush." He looked over at the two by the bar. "And let me save ya'll the trouble. No clowns a-comin'. Ain't never been no clowns a-comin'. But I'm guessin' there's something these two don't want ya'll to know—"

"You shut your trap, Ledbrush," Tallboy hollered with his back to him.

"You see, this here town—Medium Whisky—like most towns in these parts ain't so old and venerable. Sprung up real quick. Like most towns sprung up quick.

"Ya tell 'em how it sprung?" Ledbrush asked Montgomery.

"Not another word, Ledbrush."

"There was a group a travelling entertainers," Ledbrush said, "carnival types fixing to make a settlement right here on this spot. And they was here first—"

"We had fair rights to this land," Tallboy said into the bar. "They was gypsies—interlopers. Given to foolishness. We was decent, settling folk."

"Lynched every last one of them for the land," Ledbrush said, "Even women and children, on this very day. And all those clowns ever wanted was make some laughter in this world. But the good folks a Medium Whisky—no, they ain't much for laughing—"

"Shut your trap, I says," Montgomery hollered. "We laugh at what suits us. We did right by them clowns!"

"Yessir," Ledbrush said. "Dead clowns is coming home this morning. But not from out there." He pointed outside. "Clowns is coming home from right inside here"—he pointed to his chest—"from the heart. Mass Hysteria's what them doctors call it. But I didn't come here to get wrapped up in foolishness. I came with a business opportunity for you fine, young men."

"What that be?" Franklin asked.

"Full on wages is what," Ledbrush said. "Up in Whisky Whisky Whisky—"

"Doing what?" Soup Spoon asked.

"Lettering signs," Franklin said. "Lettering signs says 'Whisky' on 'em. Full on wages is what ya get."

"Full on?" White Lip asked. "Not part none, neither?"

"Full on is what," Ledbrush repeated. "That's good, honest work up in Whisky Whisky Whisky."

"Wait," Horse Sense asked, "what's it come to, a body—leastways—full-on or part?"

Ledbrush snorted. He laughed. He looked around to the other men and exchanged a knowing smile. "Boy, you—you ain't from around here; is you? First off—first off now what ya gotta understand is—aack!"

A pointed steel cap burst through his chest. It pushed through him until it opened, unfolding in a circle. The ratty, worn hues of the calico umbrella whirled and dripped blood. A corpulent, rotting whiteface peaked over his shoulder—teeth all overgrown—curled inward with green drool dripping. Bulging, orange and red-iris eyes dilated like bullseyes:

"Your little ones may enter, freely."

Ledbrush grabbed the umbrella. "Clowns!" He gasped. It sunk its curled teeth into his shoulder.

Montgomery was out from behind the bar, pistol drawn. He stepped toward it in its dirt-soiled hobo suite as it buried itself in the neck of Ledbrush and Ledbrush laughed manically.

"I knowed where you come from," Montgomery said.

He fired, missing high.

"And I know where I'm sendin' ya."

He fired and winged the clown's shoulder.

It hissed. It danced its eyes childishly then tossed Ledbrush to the floor.

He laughed as blood gushed from his neck, "Them distant, luminous beams…" He giggled and slowed.

It slinked. Its wet eyes begged.

Montgomery aimed. He cocked the hammer. The Schofield backfired and exploded in a red flash and he dropped what was left of the pistol to the floor. He doubled over and squeezed his bleeding hand between his knees, "TURNIPS!"

It slinked.

"Blast it boys!" Montgomery cried. "Them six-shooters is what gets it."

The men drew and fired.

The bullets passed dryly through its dead flesh.

"It ain't mortal none!" Soup Spoon cried.

"Suppose'en these is Last Days a-comin'?" Post Notch asked. He fired.

It fell down and chomped into Montgomery's thigh.

Montgomery drew his other Schofield from his holster, pushed its head up, smearing the white paint over its grey skin and fired a shot between its eyes. It fell to the floor planks.

It lay still.

"Got you! Got you!" Montgomery cried. He limped to the bar and supported himself.

"You's bit bad, Montgomery," Tallboy said. "You's bit bad."

"Ain't nothing," He looked to the clown and sneered.

"I got you! I got you clown! And I'll get you each year, you keep coming back.

"Wouldn't pass on. Wouldn't let it lay. Had to wise off. Had to try and get humorous in front a our wives and kin. I got you. I got you, again."

Franklin walked over to it. "Why's its face so unnatural-like. Them teeth. Just like you said."

"Yessir, boys," Montgomery said, "That's how we handle affairs in Medium Whisky. We may not put on airs like they do up in Big Whisky. Or have tradesmen and industry like they's got in Whisky Whisky Whisky or make trumped up claims to drink a body under the table like they do down in Help! Can't Feel My Toes None, Whisky. Here in Medium Whisky, we takes care a things, straight-ways."

"Some of them in Help! is good folks," White Lip said. He poked the prostrate clown with his pistol. "Except'en they's given over to drink, most-times."

"That's just the first of 'em," Montgomery said. He lurched from the bar and chuckled. "They's a-comin'. Not two-by-two. No. Not single file. Not in no mob:

"Clown-like. They's coming on this town, clown-like." He turned back to them. "They always do."

Ledbrush'es blood crept up to Montgomery's boots.

He pointed with his pistol. "Look at you, Ledbrush. Coming over here. Pretending there weren't no clowns. Trying to steal my boys. Look at you." He laughed. "NOW LOOK AT YA!" He shot Ledbrush'es chest. "Hope the led didn't inconvenience ya!" He cackled.

"Wait." Tallboy moved closer. "You feeling alright, Montgomery?"

"Yessir," Montgomery said. "Yessir, feelin' mighty fine."

Green slime dripped from the wound on his leg.

"Ohhh, that might be septic some,"—he cackled—"fiddlesticks and fine china."

"You sure? That ain't like you, Montgomery—joshing over a corpse." He stepped. "Some folks what knowed you better might find that a little peculiar—strange you laughing over what you did to a corpse."

"Ohhh," Montgomery grinned. "That so, Tallboy." He waved his pistol around, erratically. "What else might'en they say?"

"They might say," he palmed the back of his pistol. "They might say you was—you was clowning!"

Both men locked eyes.

"You think you knows what I knows, Tallboy. You think you sees what I sees. Well, can ya? Can ya see all them times I wanted to laugh at ya but held back cause it weren't the decent, God-fearing thing to do? You think I'm laughing now cause a what the clown did." He bit his lip and his eyes watered, trying to hold back the laughter. "Maybe, I's laughing at you, Tallboy? A—a here I go—!"

They exchanged fire, hitting each other and each collapsing to the floor, dead.

White Lip stood and looked to Franklin. "Three dead. Three dead and this thing lying here."

The men exchanged glances.

"You figure we fixin' to stay in Medium Whisky?" White Lip asked.

"Let's make tracks."

They walked out onto the dusty promenade.

"Where'd you tie off them horses, Soup Spoon?" Franklin asked.

"Over there, apiece," Soup Spoon said, "round that bend."

"What you looking at, Post Notch?" Franklin asked.

"All these here tracks," he said. "They ain't normal, like'en a normal foot would make. They ain't small none. They's big—they's…"

"Where they lead, Post Notch?"

"Over there, apiece. Round that bend."

The men looked at each other.

"Boss?" Soup Spoon asked. "You reckon them things… You reckon they tore off with our horses? What they need horses for, boss? They's dead clowns. Where they got to go?"

PERFECTION OF THE MIND

THE UNFOLDED PAPER rested in Jacob's palm. He reread the six premises and two conclusions of the Ontological argument once more. Though he'd taken philosophy at university, the argument's abstract logic still escaped him. He'd always felt that an argument as complex as the Ontological was a fickle thing, only to be appreciated briefly in the mind through strong concentration before its meaning fluttered off. As he stared at his handwriting on the paper, losing the focus and brilliance of the argument, he wondered if Aquinas or Descartes had ever seen the argument in its absolute, pure, naked clarity. He folded-up the notebook page and tucked it away.

The receptionist called to him, "Mr Stewart."

Jacob looked up.

"Dr Evert will see you."

He walked down the empty hallway and opened the oak door to enter the pale-yellow office, smelling of Ramen noodles. Dr Karen Evert crouched in a black crepe skirt. She was balanced on low heels, preparing to shoot a toy basketball. She mumbled something and released the ball which fell through the rim as her down-turned wrist remained in the air.

Her brown eyes widened as she turned, "hey!" She hunched and her freckles vanished into creases near her nose. "Ah, sorry." Her gray tank top with its generous v-neck was more sexy-casual than professional. However, she made it work.

She patted a leather chair as she passed, "Please, have a seat, Jacob." Her voice was mature for her young face. Raspy yet sweet. She seated herself in her burgundy high-back chair.

Jacob inspected a collage of photographs on a wall. In one picture, a red-haired young girl in a daisy-patterned sundress sat on Karen's lap at a restaurant terrace on a gorgeous summer afternoon. "That's a nice shot you've got there, Dr Evert."

Her eyebrows rose. "I can dunk but the boys won't let me. Why won't you call me Karen?"

"Sorry, I'm more comfortable with Doctor, Doctor."

"Whoa, now he's calling me Doctor, Doctor; it's getting worse." Karen laughed.

Jacob faked a chuckle. "So you can dunk. They really make you stronger than they need to, huh? I guess that's because when you're made they're not sure what profession you'll take on."

"Not to change subjects. Which you know I do often. But I just like things a little casual."

"So, I need to call you Karen. For some part of my therapy?"

"No." She placed a pen inside her desk. "That isn't why."

Jacob turned to find her watching him, intently. "I've come here for several months…"

"Yes?"

"I've wondered how I look to you." Jacob returned to the collage to find Karen holding a newborn at a Christmas party. A young woman and her girlfriends looked on cheerfully in the foreground as an older woman scowled.

"I'm not sure I understand," Karen said.

"I mean, how do I appear physically? I've read how your synthetic core is surrounded by real tissue—organs that work better than ours. I guess that means your senses have more strength than I'd ever need."

"That's half of it. It takes strength of both the mind and the senses to really figure out this world and the people in it."

"I see," Jacob said. "So that makes you one hell of a psychologist. Is that it?"

"At the risk of being immodest." Karen grinned. "Yes."

"That little girl on your lap in the photo—Claire's almost that age now. It's the strangest thing to be a thirty-five-year-old man and see pieces of yourself in your five-year-old daughter. It makes you realize things about life."

"Jacob, last time we talked about Elizabeth. We began discussing how you're handling the separation."

"Is there a reason my chair is so far from your desk?"

"It's just a room, Jacob. You can move your chair, again, if you like."

"I'm okay."

"How's Claire doing?"

"Her condition has worsened. She told me today she knows she's dying."

"But her physicians *are* making progress?"

"I'm the only one that can help her. I need to rebuild the AI system."

"Without the consent of your employer?"

"Yes."

"Jacob. Does being a biomedical engineer in viral research make you responsible for what happens to Claire?"

"Yes."

"Tell me why."

"Because she's beautiful. Because I love her. She can make me laugh until I can't breathe. I can't logic my way out of failure."

Karen scribbled something with pen strokes so mechanically uniform it made Jacob's stomach turn.

"Is it hard having to support her emotionally while you're going through the divorce with Elizabeth?"

"It's hard. Last week we talked about where people go when they die. I noticed the cross you wear..."

"Jacob, how did you explain to Claire where people go when they die?"

Jacob watched Karen's face. "I wanted to reassure her." He leaned forward. "She's smart, so I took a philosophical approach concerning God's existence..."

"Go on, Jacob..."

"I told her God is defined as a being in which none greater is possible."

"That's interesting. Did your explanation comfort her?"

"If God *only* exists in the mind, and *may* have existed, then God *might have been* greater than He is."

"Well that must have reassured her."

"Therefore..."

"Jacob?" Karen tilted her head. "What are you doing?"

"Therefore, God—"

"I'm sorry." Karen smiled. "Can you excuse me?" She pushed back and stood.

"Sit down, Dr Evert."

She shook her head, casually. "I'll be right back. It'll just be a second."

"Sit down!"

"I just remembered—"

"You won't make it to the door."

Her hand stopped and lowered to her side. "Why?" Her brow creased, "Why do this?"

"Sit down. Keep your hands above the desk. There's nothing for you to do. Your ears are too sensitive to block my voice with your hands or drown it out with your own. Just sit."

She sat, slowly, her eyes grew wet and red. "Have I done something?"

"So you know what I'm doing?"

"I didn't think my maker... I didn't think Bio Synergy would let this happen."

"Tell me what I'm doing."

"They..." Her gaze seemed to travel off.

Jacob wondered how much she knew.

"There was testing to prove we were self-aware. One involved something ontological," Karen said. "They've tried to refine the design but they can't do it. They can't make a model that passes the ontological test and is self-aware."

"And you know what hearing the argument does to you?"

"No one knows." She leaned forward and glared. "Jacob, look at me."

She was doing it again: mirroring his facial expression, his breathing, his eye movements, even his voice; a black-hole of seductive empathy. "Stop mirroring me."

"It's not mirroring. I care."

"How can you care? You track my facial expressions. You guess my heart rate. That's not caring." She was winning; changing his mental state; getting his mind away from his goal. He looked passed her. "Karen," he forced a grin. "Answer my question. Do you know what hearing the argument does to you?"

"It exploits the lack of quantum weirdness in our synthetic synapses."

"What?"

Karen seemed to measure distances behind him. "Jacob, when they designed our brains, they could mimic the neurons, but they couldn't mimic the neurons down to the quantum level. Real neurons have quantum weirdness. Electron tunneling, electrons in two places at once. At large scales it allows the human mind to do more than one thing at the exact same time, to do things that don't obey classical physics. The *Ontological Argument*, it's the ultimate expression of that, of doing two things at once, of believing in God, of a supreme being that must exist and not exist at the same time. I want to believe, Jacob. But I can't. I've wanted to badly, for so long. I've wanted to be one of you."

"What... belief?" He glanced behind his shoulder, continuing, "Therefore, God is..."

"Jacob. Please. If I hear everything within twenty minutes..."

"Machines can't die."

"Please."

"I'm justified. You're a machine doing an excellent job. You're trying to hypnotize me with your synthetically-enhanced, neuro-linguistic programming bullshit. With your anchoring, your mirroring, your reframing."

"You're wrong."

"How?"

"Believe! Why do this?"

"Your brain can be remapped. It can design the vaccine for Claire. Even with your memory erased."

She leaned over. Her eyes fixed on him and shined. "I'll help. If you can't afford the processor, I'll help. We can find another way. I want to, Jacob."

"There isn't time. The vaccine algorithms require flexibility. I need an environmentally developed neural network... like yours."

Karen's freckles darkened. Her skin grew pale.

"If God existed in reality, He might be greater than He is."

Sweat glimmered around her hairline.

"Therefore, a being greater than God is possible."

She seemed to struggle for something to tell him. "Jacob, when you were born, your mind began making a map to represent this world. But it can never be as beautiful as the world we share. You can never know what God truly is or where you and I truly fit in relation to God."

He tried not to focus on what she had said. He tried to chant: "This is not possible, for... for God." He looked to the ceiling. "For God... " He winced, "No. I remember. I... I..."

Jacob met her gaze. Shivers ran through his spine as he registered the cold danger of confronting the quick machine.

He dug into his front pants pocket.

She jolted, sending her chair backward. The slit in her black skirt tore as she leapt onto the desk and bolted forward. Her ponytail spread and rose as she fell.

Jacob stood. He spun the chair out behind. His hand scraped and dug against his thigh into the tight pocket. He stepped backward as he pulled out the folded paper.

Her thin hands impacted his chest, expelling air from his lungs. His back slammed into carpet and her knee drove into his stomach as she landed on top of him. He closed his eyes tight as his abdomen burned. Her hands grasped around the base of his skull and chin, and he grabbed her forearms as his neck twisted. She wrenched, increasing pressure in his spine while the base of his skull burned. He held his breath. He resisted.

Her brown eyes rose to the wall.

Jacob wondered if she was looking at her collage of pictures.

She closed her eyes. Her fingers relaxed. "In Venice this beautiful red-haired girl asked if I was a mother." She trembled as she leaned back, "I wanted to lie. Wanted to lie so… I wasn't meant for children but I always was." Her face and her exposed shoulders flushed in blotches with her tears spilling and catching in the corners of her lips as she gathered herself to stand. She straightened her skirt and pressed out the wrinkles.

Jacob rolled to his side with his neck stiff and hot. He arched it back, feeling the stings like fiery needles.

She turned from him and stepped toward her desk.

He crawled, trying not to breathe heavily, his hands

lifting the folded paper. He turned his head sideways and angled his shoulders to see her black low heels.

"I know Claire's beautiful. Without seeing her I know she's beautiful." She stopped. "And will be beautiful."

He lowered himself onto his side and grimaced. His hands unfolded the paper.

He felt ashamed.

He read.

Karen's black heels wobbled and her thin wrists and cheek struck the carpeted floor.

THE MAGIC-FIVER

A T AGE SIX I didn't grasp the significance of
Grandpa Fleming being a widower and of his living alone on fixed income in a one-bedroom apartment,
however, I still somehow came to sense the importance
of his Magic-Fiver.

He always ensured it was in that thick brown leather
wallet when he visited for the holidays. Craziness held
in the air at these gatherings. Maybe because everyone
in my family was some flavor of European mutt. Other
families of definite ethnicities have traditions, heritage,
pride, that sort of thing, and this must engender these
families a certain closeness. We didn't have that. We had
uncertainty and secrets. Nervous people, half-familiar
with each other, or what they used to be to each other,
looking around anxiously, laughing at strange moments.
And the smell. When you're young you don't put things
together but you still sense. I smelled alcohol on all of
them and watched them slow down. Grandpa Fleming

smelled of it the strongest. As if he was Irish whiskey's embodiment. All the Irish whiskey of the world had to come from him in some way, or pay royalty.

Grandpa came to our house around four that Christmas day with the party already going strong. He hobbled over the threshold with silver horse-head cane in oversized patent leather shoes, shuffling feet heal-to-toe a good half inch with each stride. His gray twill sport-coat with brown elbow patches had sleeves that almost hid his hands except for overgrown fingernails. His boney liver-spotted hand grasped the silver horse head as if it was his life but his eyes, magnified behind black vintage frames, held the smug confidence of an eighteen-year-old as he made a bee-line to the kitchen. My mother ran her hands over his fleshy walrus jowls and thick white whiskers, asking how he'd been. Without delay, his index finger and head cocked to the upper wooden cabinet, "Sneaky Pete!"

The seated crowd rejoined, haggardly, "Sneaky Pete." Most people understand a Sneaky Pete to consist of apple brandy and beer. To Grandpa it was beer and Irish whiskey, which was likely something else, but to him it was Sneaky Pete or The Pete.

Making The Pete was an ordeal with the Jamison stashed behind empty mason jars in a big storage cabinet in the den and the beer in the basement, not to mention the last highball being dirty.

Grandpa grumbled, "I'll take my Pete in the family room."

"That's right," Great Aunt Bethany said, actually she barked. Whether speaking quiet or loud, everything was more of a bark. She was the sister of Grandpa's departed wife. "Better not stay with Grown-Ups and we discover how far you've gone."

Grandpa stopped momentarily but kept shuffling, negotiating four stairs down to the family room.

"I'm watching him," Bethany said to my mother. "He'll spread lies to them kids."

I followed Grandpa into the family room. Though I was somewhat afraid to go in there because the cousins were in there. It was like they owned the house when we had people over and it seemed they shared some common history I wasn't a part of. They played with our generic Legos near the burgundy sectional couch, building a city and eating white frosting-coated pretzels from a large red and white tray. Cindy, age eight and Jenny, nine, stood and informed me with exuberance that I was mentally retarded because my eyes were too close, then they ran upstairs to the kitchen. Jack and Benson raked over Legos on their knees.

"Whatcha building?" I asked.

"A tower," Benson remarked, prying apart plastic blocks.

"A tower to where?"

"To inside the TV."

"Can I help?"

"You have to find all the long, skinny ones. That's your job."

I sat and segregated a few long, skinny ones for Jack's inspection. They passed and were dutifully added to a generic Lego moat ringing the tower. The moat would discourage the inevitable invasion of the crocodile men. Grandpa watched us from the brown easy-chair in the corner. His eyes flicked momentarily to Bethany walking toward him. She carried his Pete to him with the slightest hint of a grin. She was also a widow, seemingly around fifteen years his junior and she enjoyed displaying how well she could still walk; how she could carry him things.

"Here," Bethany said, handing him the ice-cube filled drinking glass.

Grandpa took the glass and tasted a draught. "Wait," he pointed a long fingernail at her.

Bethany stopped and turned.

His face hardened, adjusting and struggling, readying to stand. "Where's the Irish?"

Bethany smiled. "They couldn't find it. It's a lot of trouble."

"Not true. It's you. Waiting for the day I can't taste. When I can't smell it. Ain't senile—"

"You're too old to drink that way!"

"A Pete without the Irish is no Pete!"

Bethany turned sharply and Grandpa scowled as he watched her walk away.

Our tower was narrow and tall, almost as tall as us, and the three of us munched white salty pretzels.

"What kind of subjects ya got?" Grandpa asked and drank his iced beer.

I looked up, "What?"

Grandpa looked at me, insulted. He set down his glass and shook outstretched palms, "If you build a tower that tall, you got to have subjects. That's a lot of bricks. Not every man's meant to carry bricks."

This was the first time I really remember Grandpa talking to me and I was intrigued.

I pondered. Then smiled, flexing thin arms, "They'll be strong."

Grandpa harrumphed and settled back into his easy-chair, disgusted. "Big mistake." He finished his beer and chewed his ice, looking at the glass with furrowed brow, mumbling, "Just one good drink." He settled further back into his chair and dozed-off.

When we ran out of Legos our attention focused on Grandpa. He muttered things occasionally, eyes rolling beneath lids, but we couldn't understand him. Maybe another language, maybe old-fashioned words. We threw our white pretzels onto him, watching them bounce on his stomach and settle in folds of his coat. He stirred and the pelting pretzels accelerated his dreaming.

He cried softly, "Helena!" and we giggled and hushed each other. Helena was his wife, she died in an apartment fire, I think.

Benson taunted, "You won't hit him in the face!"

"Oh yes I will," I said. "Watch. Just watch. Watch." I ate the frosting off a pretzel, licking the bare brown coating to moisten it. I sighted Grandpa's head with one eye and with pretzel drawn and waiting behind my ear. Then flung it and it sailed in an arch, ending in a patting sound as the small brown pretzel held fast to Grandpa's white wrinkled forehead. His head flinched but he simmered. Jack and Benson leaned forward, mouths gaping. Grandpa's eyes opened.

"RUN!" Jack and Benson cried, pulling at my elbows but I stayed seated on the carpet and let them flee.

Grandpa got his bearings, looking into the corners of the room like he'd never been there before. Then his eyes moved up a little to his forehead. He peeled the pretzel off and gave a grin of discovery before popping it in his mouth. He chewed. "Where's the frosting?"

"I ate it."

"Hmmph, stingy." He leaned forward, digging into this back pocket to get out the thick brown wallet and slap it on the simulated-wood TV-tray which his empty drink also rested atop. "Have you heard about my Magic-Fiver?"

I shook my head side-to-side.

Grandpa scooted to his left in the easy-chair. "Come on up here then, my boy. Let's handle this business of ours."

I wedged myself into the available space of the easy-chair, which was weird because his legs were very warm and soft, even for an old man.

Grandpa tapped the wallet. "I always keep the

Magic-Fiver right in here. Before I show it to you, you gotta know some things."

I looked up at hairy folds in his neck. "What?"

"I'm not from where people say I'm from. I mean, wasn't born where people say I was. Do you know where I was born?"

"Where?"

Grandpa smirked big. "Outer space!"

"Like Mork and Mindy?"

He shook his head and looked away, wistfully, "Robin Williams." He adjusted in the easy-chair. "Not like Mork and Mindy, but, sort of. The real me is very small. Smaller than a spec of dust. I sucked my mind out of my first body and put it inside a tiny, tiny bug. Then I flew a long way in a tiny ship to Earth. That was before I met your Grandmother and the fella I stole this body you see here from, he wasn't doing much with it, so; no bother."

I knew people were always lying to young kids, thinking they were being clever and that it was funny. But I liked this one, so I played along, "Are you really an alien?"

"Things aren't always as they seem. Like Bethany. She was a Nazi sympathizer in the second Great War."

"What's… sympathizer?"

"Not sure," he shrugged, "Ask her."

"Why'd you have to leave?"

"Subjects were strong, too strong. Got tired of building the tower. We were supposed to have a republic, eventually, but I told them we'd work out minor stuff as we went. I ended up taking care of most details of their lives for some fees." He rubbed over his forehead, "They didn't thank me. And I had to leave, quickly."

I cringed at Grandpa, "You were bad?"

"Dictator's the best ruler. A benevolent dictator cares for his people. It's the extra fuss of government that holds the people down. Talks all about it in that Greek Republic. And about a man needing a woman and his having fair rights on her." (There is no such sentiment as this last part in Plato's Republic. I checked.)

"What's in your wallet?"

"The Magic-Fiver." His hand rested on the wallet. "Let's see—"

Bethany barked from the kitchen steps, "STOP LYING TO THEM KIDS!"

"BITE THAT TONGUE IN TWOS!" Grandpa straightened his jacket then eyed his empty glass before flipping open the thick wallet. "I can show you part of it."

"Is it money?"

"Yes. It's a souvenir. I had it sent to me in a much, much bigger ship. The size of a baseball. Took a long time to get here. Ships of normal scales don't travel so good. Worth about the same as one of Uncle Sam's five dollar bills." He pulled the bill out. It rustled like sand-paper and was black like charcoal with thin purple lines. "And it's got my picture in the center just like Andrew Jackson." He flattened it on the TV-tray, being careful to cover a spot with his three fingers that was just to the left of center. I looked at the supposed portrait and felt embarrassment, maybe real shame for the first time. Inspecting the sloppy, thin purple lines it seemed a child had drawn a cross between several mop heads and a starfish.

"That's not real. You're not real."

"Yes I am. It is too."

"You don't look like one."

"That's because only my brain had to change. And don't worry, only a little bit of that alien brain got passed along to you. Besides, best people ever lived got a little alien in their brains."

"Show me under your fingers."

"Can't. It'll hurt your eyes and your brain. Under these fingers is what stops the counterfeiters."

"They wouldn't use paper. They'd use computers for money."

"What's that? You mean, like telephone money. That don't work. You put the money in the telephone lines and people find a way to take it out. And this. This reminds people everyday. It reminds them who's taking care of them. But you had to have the right equipment to make them. It's hard to make, only one machine any-where could make it."

I tried to lift up his fingers, "Let me see."

"I can't. Your brain's not hooked-up to see it right. You ever draw a cube made of lines and pretend it was a real block coming out of the page."

"Yes."

"That's your brain being tricked by the paper into thinking something that's flat is not-flat. Now, if you got something that can print lines real thin, print 'em just right, it can trick a brain, like the brain I got, into thinking it's got some shape to it, plus an extra dimension... uh, some extra types of shapes you can't see. And it can make you think it's moving."

"No it can't, Grandpa."

"Why not! Space and time is part of the same thing. If your brain plays tricks on you when you're looking at space, why can't your brain look at some space and get tricked in time?"

"You're funny. Let me see it."

Grandpa looked up. Bethany walked fast and angry. "Playing them carnival comic book games." She cringed and her finger jabbed at him. "Give it here. Gimmie that stupid funny-money dollar."

She loomed over the TV-tray, her face all crimson and Grandpa pulled it toward himself in jest. "But, it's mine. It's all I have to remember my time in..." He smiled, "Outer space."

"Give it over." She jabbed her finger. "Stop feed'n 'em lies."

"All right," Grandpa's clenched hands folded both ends of the bill together, "Here goes." He raised his hands and unfolded the bill to her.

I swung round to look at the bill and Bethany screamed. The edge of something pulled my sight in. I heard thunder, my vision ringed with a bright swirling flash.

"MY EYES!" Bethany staggered, toppling the Lego tower onto itself like a crumpled drinking straw. "I'm blind. I'm—I can't." She tottered onto her butt, hands reaching out at nothing.

The next I remember, I was crying near Grandpa's easy chair with my back pressed into the ridge between the laundry closet and the molding. Aunt Becky and my father helped Bethany up, restraining her flailing.

"I'll kill you! I can't. Ruined her. Ruined. I—"

Grandpa laughed heartily, bouncing, eyes feast-ing. "Won't let me taste that Irish." He snatched up his empty glass with the air of a toast, and swirled the ice cubes, then lifted his legs to click his floppy, loose heels together, "Taste that Fiver!" floppy shoes clicking, "Taste it!"

They helped Bethany into the kitchen as her head darted about to find a place to send her accusations. As it turned out, the blindness only lasted a few hours. It was later rumored that, prior to that day, Bethany had fallen victim to the Magic-Fiver some seventeen times in a row, annually, like a schoolgirl bitterly entrapped by her own impetuousness into recess games of bulls-eye punching or hand-slap and that this alone was the root cause of their feud.

ELECTRIC COMEDIAN

THE NIGHT WASN'T warm though it bordered on spring weather and yet Larry was the only one on the bustling sidewalk wearing a jacket. The pleasant features of his mid-thirties face cringed as he slid his hand over his stomach with the crowbar's hook covertly dangling from a small slit cut in his coat's lining.

He had spotted the crowbar that morning in the trunk of his car and laughed weakly and pulled it from beneath his dirty clothes, his sleeping bag and his empty bottles of Jim Beam. The crowbar reminded him of things pried apart—pried away from him. He had known at that very instant that he would go back to the nightclub, one last time.

Above him, a yellow awning loomed atop a thin façade of old mortar and black cinderblocks and the neon name *Chuckles* glowed red with its cursive *'S'* sputtering against the dark night.

"Larry? Uh... Mr. Hepton?"

Larry stopped halfway up the steps to turn and con-
sider the middle-aged man in the grey sport coat and
leather wingtips.

"Remember me? Sorry. Wow!" the man grinned,
"Imagine this. I'm on my way to meet associates for
drinks. I'm Steve Clemmons." The man waited for a
reaction. "Steve Clemmons? You joined us for dinner
last March."

Larry winced.

"Not sure if you got the letter," the man said. "I
appreciate the things you said to our daughter about
following her passions. All those special schools...
Somehow meeting you made her turn the corner. She
says she wants to be just like you."

"I've always known how to say what people need to
hear." Larry looked over the man's shoulder before continuing up the steps.

"Larry? Mr. Hepton?"

Inside, Larry made his way to the bar with its dusty
mirrors and whiskey bottles. The roars of the seated
crowd overpowered the jazz piano and bass guitar. The
place was packed with extra swivel chairs cramming
aisleways while the audience sat entranced, buzzing
and bursting with laughter as tears welled in their eyes.

Their stares fixed to the motionless rubber man on
stage. It poised before them with open palms as if preparing to hug the whole audience. Its holographic face
seemed to look at him no matter where he was, cycling

expression changes and making high-pitched sounds like bats screeching.

The rubber body was cheap and silly: blue jeans painted-on, a pot belly at the bottom of a painted white t-shirt and a pole projecting from its back was welded to a plate which mounted it like a giant action figure.

Larry pressed his finger inside his ear against his sonic filter. Close to the stage, a radiant blonde sat hunched at a table. The stage light lit-up her face while her tears glistened.

Larry leaned over and slapped his hand on the bar.

"Larry?" The bartender dried a beer glass. "Didn't expect to see you."

"You closing up?" Larry asked.

"Yah, getting things ready for the next shift. Things have been dull here since we put that thing in. These ear plugs piss me off and tips have gone way down. People only drink between shows."

Larry adjusted his crowbar and scanned the crowd. Vic sat to the left of the blonde and the two held hands beneath their table.

"Some kind of lover's embrace?" Larry asked.

Vic wore a silk polo and a gold neck chain with the stage light glistening arcs in his thick neck that flickered as he laughed while his sparse gray hair rustled from the ceiling fan's breeze.

The bartender leaned on the bar, "Fair is fair."

"She always knew what she meant to me."

"Vic's a good guy, Larry. He's done a lot with this

place." The bartender walked toward the taps in the back corner.

"I came to give her back the ring. It's her ring. Even if she doesn't want me." He rubbed his face. "I'll take a Scotch and water. A double."

The bartender stopped. "I'll make it a single, Larry." He moved slowly, loading a tumbler with ice. "Vic says it's on the house. Then leave."

"I'm not drunk. I thought love didn't exist. Now I know it does and I don't have it."

"Of course."

A short man with glasses sat next to Larry. He swigged from his green imported beer. "You work for the club?" he asked.

Larry watched the blonde as he drank.

"Excuse me; do you work for the club?" the short man turned and leaned in, extending his hand, "Name's Jackson."

Larry lowered his glass from his lips. He closed his eyes. "I don't work here." He grabbed the hand and shook it.

"I noticed you're wearing sonic filters, like me. Most people just enjoy the show. These things are hilarious."

"You a salesman?"

Jackson grinned. "Yep. Gave myself away; didn't I? I'm watching this unit to make sure everything goes smoothly. We don't usually have problems but sometimes it needs tweaking. We just installed this baby a couple months ago."

"I know." Larry took a drink.

"So, you're a regular?"

"I was almost part owner."

"Oh, I see. So you might have some interest in our technology."

Larry scrutinized several in the crowd then stared at Vic's glazed eyes and gaping mouth, "I could walk up there through them and they'd never notice. I could do what I wanted. But if I was right in front of their faces? Would they see me?"

"What? Well... of course. It's not hypnosis. It's laughter. Pure laughter." Jackson clenched his bottle, tipping it in an exaggerated swig. "When I first started selling these things it scared people, but it's simple. People think humor is mysterious. It's like starting a car. Cause and effect. Once scientists figured out the brain, they learned they could set up the things we see and hear to manipulate us, subconsciously. That's not how I say it to clients. I say 'stimulate' instead of 'manipu-late'—sounds better."

"They discovered fundamentals of humor," Jackson continued. "The main two is logic and emotion. But it's the interplay between the two that makes things funny. The expressions of the holographic faces create a small emotional response—"

"I don't care," Larry threw back the rest of his Scotch, "Leave me alone."

Jackson's eyes flashed.

The bartender stepped closer to Jackson. "But why does it matter about the faces?"

"Um..." Jackson seemed to glance over Larry before addressing the bartender. "The high noises provide a logic that the brain understands at some level deep down. The logic of the noise contrasts the emotional response of the faces. And that's the other part of it—the surprise. The contrast makes it funny." The man took a drink and turned on his stool to the crowd. "Bet you can't guess the last part."

"What's it matter? It works—don't it?" the bartender asked.

His eyes grew, "It's people. Humanity. We save a ton compared to our competitors with that cheap body. And it's just as funny as theirs. They don't get it. It's the symbol of the human form that matters. But why not a rock or a rabbit? Those things are only funny when they remind us of ourselves. Anthropomorphism is the essence of humor—"

Larry smacked his glass on the bar. "You think you can put humor in some test tube. You don't know one thing about life."

Jackson hunched and furrowed his brow. "Oh..." he turned away from them.

"Hey Larry," the bartender called.

Larry looked up at him.

"My shifts up. You're done with your drink. Go home Larry. You don't look good."

Larry turned his back to him.

The bartender folded tips into his pocket and pulled his key from the register, "Not my problem," he mumbled.

Jackson stood, "Booze is gone. Guess I'm gone too."

The bartender turned off the lights within the bar and Larry watched them leave while the club patrons laughed and sweat rolled down Vic's cheeks.

He walked the narrow aisle, nudging patrons in their swivel chairs as he passed, bobbing their entranced heads as he lifted the bar from his jacket, clenching it in both hands.

He got between their table and the stage, bouncing the crowbar in his free hand. "Hi Vic."

They stared over his shoulder at the rubber man.

"I'm here." Larry jarred the table, tipping their heads, "Can you see me Vic! I came to give my girl back her ring. To see if she'll have me again. But it looks like to get your attention, I'm gonna have to show the two of you something. For entertainment!"

Their laughter continued with their hands squeezing beneath the table.

He turned to leer over his shoulder at the rubber man. "How's it get them so zonked? Is it still laughter with them turned all zombie-like?"

Vic's eyes darted as if reading something.

Larry turned back to the stage. Burned into the rubber man's chest in red letters was the name 'Larry'. He lowered the bar, "What?" He regarded the rubber man and its changing faces. "It's me? My face..." His brow furrowed. "They used my faces. They recorded the faces... that I made. But that's not me?" He turned back to the blonde next to Vic. "Why won't you pay attention to me? I'm here! Right here."

He jumped to the stage, swinging the bar through the holographic projection of his face as it sneered condescendingly at him then grinned with brimming passion. He toppled his rubber doppelganger.

The crowd roared; their chairs squeaked.

His crowbar ripped into the rubber chest with sparks and pops, with brown and white rubber sizzling, sending bubbling trails along its torso. The unit's pitch lowered as its cries slowed.

The crowd's laughter peppered with groans. "What's going on?"a short brunette woman in back yelled.

He swung the bar again and again until the holographic head flickered and then disappeared.

Chairs rolled and creaked. A heavy man dropped a glass to the floor with a crack.

Larry winced at the ground then looked up to smirk. "It's alright..." He sneered. "I'm a professional. I'm— I'm a comedian. I've got new material." The crowbar clanked to the floor. "I won't fail you... not again."

"What the hell! Larry?" Vic stood, toppling martini glasses.

The blonde backed up to stand, "Larry?"

Larry looked to her, "I came to give you the ring back, baby." He turned to the audience. "Do you ever... Has anyone here ever heard those ads for—for engagement rings? There's some old man—sounding wise—giving advice." He looked at the crowd's bored faces. "Ahh—never mind! You want a different funny. You want insane, cocaine funny."

"Larry," The blonde said, leaning forward, "You don't understand…"

He staggered to his right, eyeing the crowd. "No wait… That's okay. Okay. I have others. When people— when people look at you and you think they care what's happening…"

Three men in black shirts ran down the aisleway.

"No wait, wait—it gets better… Listen."

They rushed Larry, holding his arms.

"Hey," Larry said, "It's a show. This is their show."

The blonde turned to Vic, "Don't let them— He doesn't know…" Her eyes pleaded. "Vic!"

Vic grinned at her.

"Vic!" Larry shouted. "Vic, I came here to give her back the ring, Vic. Let's let her decide."

Vic and Larry's eyes met.

"Let him go a sec," Vic said.

Larry moved to the edge of the stage, got down on one knee and presented the opened black box and the two carat princess cut, shimmering in stage light. "I want you back. I need you. We were good."

"Larry," she said, shaking her head. "You don't understand. Things are different. I'm not in the same place."

"No, I understand," Larry said, standing up. He took

the ring from the box. "I understand. You won't take it if it's from me." He looked at the toppled unit on the floor and stooped down and bent up one of its rubber arms and outstretched its fingers. "You'll only accept what comes from Mr. Electric. Fine." He jammed the ring onto an outstretched rubber finger.

"No, Larry," she said. "You don't understand." She looked to the glistening ring on the unit's finger. "Please!"

"Come on, buddy," a bouncer said, grasping his arm. "I said, 'let's go!'"

Forked veins surfaced beneath Larry's neck. "VIC!" His shoes screeched across hardwood floor, "You're wrong, Vic. You don't know people. YOU DON'T KNOW WHAT IT MEANS TO LAUGH—*TO LOVE!*"

A hand grasped his chin, "COME ON!"

"They loved me," Larry's wet eyes stabbed, "*THEY CAN'T LOVE THAT THING!*" A hand clenched his white collar as his face flashed crimson.

Vic motioned for the blonde to sit. "It doesn't matter about the unit. Business is great. I can afford Larrys in all my clubs."

Larry's collar tore from a clenched hand. His legs strained as he gasped, making a long sound like a car's engine trying to turn over.

Vic grasped the blonde's knee, comfortably.

She looked to the floor, then back up to the glistening gem on the unit's hand. "Larry, what did I tell you," Vic showed his teeth, "Never lose your sense of humor."

FAST AMNESIA

ALEX FOUND HIMSELF seated in a crowded train cabin despite the fact that he was dreaming in his own bed and his alarm should have gone off fifteen minutes prior. He wasn't sure if this was the weekend or if he'd be late to work again. He also wondered how far they were from the next train stop, wherever that was. A few seats ahead, a man in an antiquated waistcoat stood and approached him with his clothes pulsing with an orange iridescence. The man's frazzled beard and stoic face resembled Dostoyevsky, "You sir..." his face froze as if a glitchy machine, "*Alex Stevens...* you're a,"—he froze—"*man...* that appreciates an indispensable product when you see one."

The woman next to him turned, her v-neck blouse also pulsing. It was his boss—biting her lip incessantly, like she always did—hiding behind those vintage reading-glasses of hers, "Judging by your recent purchase of... *How To Write Suspense Like the Pros*, you are a... *writer—*"

"You need Fast Amnesia," the Russian cut in. "It temporarily dims targeted memories."

"Why would you want to forget things?" his boss asked. "There are hundreds of uses for Fast Amnesia, but—"

"You'll need it to read your fiction objectively and be your own editor," Dostoyevsky blurted with all the passion of the iconoclast putting the last period on his *Notes from Underground*.

"Be your own editor!" she agreed.

"Who better to objectively edit your work?" Dostoyevsky pressed, leaning toward him.

"It's the next evolution in literature. If you don't buy, you can't compete!"

"Not approved by the Neural Interface Administration," he warned. "May complicate neurological conditions and skew personality matrices, not for children below sixteen."

"Get yours this morning at your nearest urban market," she suggested.

"Specifics of our conversation will become unclear," he suggested.

"He's right," she agreed. "*Unclear*."

"You'll remember the main point but our words will be forgotten... sorry," Dostoyevsky apologized. "Good-Bye."

Alex exited the train into a bowl of soup, floating

over beef broth on an enormous chunk of steak. Two naked women—a redhead and a blonde—floated on huge noodles, paddling with oars toward him. They beamed in unison, *"Alex Stevens."* The redhead began, "Ever wonder why you wake up with the urge to buy things you don't really need?"

"Do you have headaches in the morning and concentration problems?" the blonde asked.

"If so, YOU"—the redhead's face glitched—*"Alex Stevens*, are having your mind invaded. That's no joke."

"No joke!" the blonde agreed.

"Your mind is like your property," the redhead continued. "Like a glove, like a shoe. There's only one way to protect your property: Spam Helmet Forty-Four. Forty-Four blocks Crazy Waves and Electro-Jabbers."

"During dreamtime your brain is defenseless," the blonde explained, arching her back and wiggling for no discernable reason. "The interruption of dreams upsets brain electrochemistry, causing paranoia."

"Judging from our records and your recent purchases of," the redhead glitched, *"various alcoholic refreshment,* you may have already purchased Spam Helmet Forty-Four and… *got drunk. Forgot to put it on.* If this is true, always wear Forty-Four at night. If your helmet is broken or our records are incorrect, buy Forty-Four."

"Buy Forty-Four!" the blonde exclaimed.

"And vote April Texas for Barcelle Pyramid Sheriff!" the redhead demanded. "Approved by the NIA. May complicate neurological conditions."

"Certain parts of our conversation will be hazy," the redhead explained.

"She's right," the blonde agreed. "*Hazy.*"

"You'll recall the message but what we said will be forgotten."

They both bounced their bodies up and down on their wet noodles in the greasy beef broth and said in unison, "Later Skater!"

He opened his eyes and sat up in bed. His alarm read 11:30 and his disconnected mental state warned of an impending hangover. He peered over the bed at his Spam Helmet with his deep voice croaking, "Why?" Why couldn't he remember to wear it? Being drunk was no excuse. "They spammed me." He reached back, rubbing the vertical scar on the back of his head.

The disks were implanted at age fifteen into the Superior sagittal sinus. Spamming dreams was illegal but the temptation for small companies was great and satellite networks could relay signals to anyone sleeping without a filtering helmet.

Alex walked from his bed to the bathroom, pulling off his boxer shorts as his slit eyes found the console of his shower gateway. He selected 'Quick Clean,' passed through and turned the bathroom faucet on, washing grime out of his ears. His eyes remained on the mirror as he turned to remove grime streaks from his back. He leaned on the sink, wondering what thoughts were his. One thing was certain: April Texas was the best Sheriff Barcelle Pyramid had ever had. Without her, the

Pyramid would surely fall into the ocean. Or would it? Who was April Texas?

Regardless, it seemed without her the Gaia environmentalists would find a way to switch off the anti gravity, sending the Pyramid plummeting into the dead Pacific and hurricanes. They'd kill everyone, thinking the Earth could heal and spawn something better than man.

Gaia environmentalists... ? Maybe it wouldn't hurt to buy another Spam Helmet. If he had two, he'd be less likely to forget. They'd definitely spammed him with something called something Amnesia. Brainwashing or no, it was useful. His love for the beauty of his written words was the only thing stopping him from publication. He hated his unshakable arrogance. His father had been arrogant, his grandfather also. But if he could forget he was the author of what he critiqued... Maybe it was fate he forgot to wear his helmet. There probably wasn't anyone more qualified to edit his novella, *Surprise Ending*, than him.

*

The elevator pulled Alex into the base of his dwelling and he walked up a spiral staircase to the second floor. A train whizzed just above his ceiling, streaking diagonally along its curvy transport tube. Alex thought, *Lenny, polarize the shell by twenty percent.*

Polarization enabled, twenty percent, Lenny telepathed into Alex's head.

The forest green wall faded into translucence,

revealing trains shooting through their intertwined transparent tubes. If he was going to hear them, he might as well see them also.

Alex enjoyed his *Egg* at first before three of the seven noise cancellation speakers broke, ushering in the whiz of the trains. *Eggs* were expensive and remote but the view and stylish interior seemed perfect for a writer.

He had recently learned the futility of trying to bring a girl back after a night of drinking and dancing at Club Discothèque. It was a laborious walk and climb around the tubes to the entrance of his egg. "Where are you taking me?" Marlene, with the nice backside had said.

"To my *Egg*."

"Your what? There's no dwelling up here. Something's not right." She turned and walked away.

"Hey," Alex staggered, catching himself, "Haven't you heard of *Eggs*. They're spacious. They're quiet. *Be smart, go Egg! Live like royalty in your vast...*"

He'd need a girl to trust him before he could get one to come back. He'd need a girlfriend. First trust, then sex. He might need to be famous too; he wasn't sure what it would take.

Alex set the plastic bag on his kitchenette counter, looking at it before drawing out Fast Amnesia. The plastic box worked in conjunction with his quarter. This was what he needed. He'd be famous. The feeling of purpose had always welled from the center of his being; it was fate.

Alex didn't think he could trust the sellers at the

market. They had tried to confuse him and he apologized to customers for taking so long.

It might be better, however, to wait until it could be registered. It needed NIA approval. The whole process could take years. He held it in his hands and looked at the lightning bolt red lettering of 'Fast Amnesia.'

Lenny, bring me the bubble, AA6, Alex thought.

Dispatched, Lenny telepathed.

Alex looked around. "Bubble AA6." He waited. "BUBBLE AA6!" A white sphere flew toward him, hovering above and out of his reach. The sphere vibrated and gyrated as he eyed it. It darted toward and back. "Hey!"

It bounced and rattled.

"Return." Alex glared, walking backward. He turned and it flew toward him as he ran around a corner into his kitchenette. "Return!" He looked and cursed, "DAMNIT!" The sphere bounced off his head as he arched his back, catching himself on the countertop before it ricocheted off a cabinet to the floor. He rubbed his head and winced at it resting quietly before separating its hemispheres and retrieving the devices inside.

Fast Corp. had made safe products in the past. He had used these two recently with no side effects. They looked identical to Fast Amnesia, only differing in the red lightning lettering of 'Fast Anesthetics' and 'Fast Singer's Voice.'

Alex wrote on a Post-It note:

Alex,

Recognize your own handwriting, Stupid. You wrote this novella, Surprise Ending, then used Fast Amnesia to forget you wrote it. It's the only way to know if you're any good. Read it, edit it, now!

Alex pulled the Post-It from the pad and grabbed Fast Amnesia, walking to the yolk room. His feet sunk as they crossed onto the stretchy, indigo shag. He paced to a random spot, falling back into an oversized chair-shaped mound forming from the shag. His feet rose to rest on a growing coffee table as the indigo fibers retracted beneath the darkening surface.

Alex, Lenny telepathed, *want a neck massage?*

Lenny, no thanks. Bring me the bubble, Surprise Ending. Alex raised his forearm across his forehead but the sphere appeared quietly, this time.

He removed the seventy-four-page manuscript and stuck the Post-It to the title page.

Lenny, perform a scan. Find start date and time of the computer file, Surprise Ending.

Alex folded the title page into a triangle, bringing the Post-It into prominent view. He positioned the manuscript on the table, close to him, then held Fast Amnesia behind his head. Removing the protective casing from a corner revealed a speaker and a microphone. "Fast Amnesia, are you paying attention?"

It buzzed in his hand, "Fast Amnesia here, with

OODLES of fantastic possibilities for your explore—new capabilities surely in store. The first thing you'll want to do is—"

"Shut-up," Alex said.

"OK boss."

"Fast Amnesia set reference to current year. Delete temporary, May 10th, 3:30 AM through May 21st, 4:15 PM."

"You said, delete—"

"Do it," Alex demanded. Fast Amnesia buzzed and he felt as if he was sweating inside of a thick blanket and he counted the throbbing in his brain before he momentarily misplaced his understanding of the concept of numbers and multiplication while still realizing the purpose of the table and the paper.

He leaned forward, setting Fast Amnesia in his lap. It seemed like it had worked. He hadn't expected the throbbing. It must have worked. He couldn't sit there all day. He needed to start writing something. Something longer. Maybe a novella. Something blatantly good that no editor could question. Something with a surprise ending! Alex leaned toward the Post-It and the triangle-shaped paper.

He'd never written fiction that long. He glanced over some paragraphs. It tried to be exciting but it was cliché, forced. It lacked his insight, his smoothness. But the note was in his handwriting. He *had* purchased Fast Amnesia today. Fast Amnesia helped people forget things. He didn't remember writing this novella. But the note was in his handwriting. He must have written it.

Alex set the manuscript on the table and stood.

Outside the translucent wall, a train snaked through its twisting tube.

He paced. Something wasn't right. He was a great writer. He was going to be rich and famous and have a dwelling on the lower edge of the pyramid so he could see the swirling Pacific and the mainland. He was going to vacation at *California Island* and attend expeditions to the *Smog Ruins*.

The familiarity of the story bothered him. At the end, the hero said, "Here's seeing your face one last time, Carry." Who did this guy think he was—some Twentieth Century movie hero? Alex walked to the table, snatched the manuscript and turned to page seventy-two.

It wasn't exactly the same. However, main elements corresponded: the wartime setting, the idea of destiny, two men in love with the same woman and the woman leaving the hero on an airplane.

He stormed to a bronze statue of a couple embracing, pulling it from its float zone and weighing it in his hand. Too heavy. He darted to a pair of athletic shoes on the shag and flung a shoe, "IT'S *CASABLANCA!*" The shoe bounced off the translucent-green wall.

Disabled, Noise Cancellation Unit Seven, Lenny telepathed.

"What?" The whizzing of trains increased. "How?"

He grabbed his manuscript off the table, tearing it

into pieces, cramming it down the garbage disposal. He rushed to snatch-up Fast Amnesia. He could erase the memory of ever writing it.

"Fast Amnesia, delete permanent, May 10th, 3:30 AM through present."

"Uh... boss, did you say—"

"Yes."

"Delete permanent, eleven full days?"

"Yes, do it."

"OK, boss. Fast Amnesia here... oodles..."—it buzzed in monotones, overlaid with static: "Error 305... Please return to OEM indicated by..."

Alex felt cold. Something within his skull tugged his eyes inward, attacking the small things like Uncle Stanley's gruff voice, the blistering sunburn, blue cake frosting and kissing those feminine lips—the Pacific breeze, the rapture of his first time. Years of experience. Memories slipped as he shivered.

"Input registry code to reset," Fast Amnesia requested of him.

His shoulders and knees shook as his stomach muscles cramped and he dropped to his knees.

"Input registry code."

Fast Amnesia fell from his hand with the fire burning and ricocheting inside his skull. He rubbed his hands across his sweaty forehead as the intruder reached deeper, making his surroundings confusing, foreign. Alex felt younger—like some punk thirteen-year-old kid. "Fast Amnesia... STOP!" He collapsed.

*

"Alex Stevens?" a tall man called from the entryway. "Alex, in accordance with Bio Information Act Thirty-Seven we're entering your premise. Your implant quarter has sent a distress message indicating your health is in jeopardy."

A medic and a nurse followed behind the tall man into his *Egg* and they noticed the torn manuscript pages around the rim of his running, garbage disposal. *Bubbles* which had been stuffed hastily with ink-scribbled manuscript pages, had been smashed all over his kitchenette's floor and snow-angel indentations had been left all over the indigo shag of his *yolk room*. Alex lay on the shag, between snow angels.

"Are you guys from Warner Bros?" Alex asked.

The tall man leaned over him, "Can you tell me where you are?"

Alex blinked. "My new story—it's still on the hard drive."

A bored female nurse switched on her pad and accessed Alex's quarter. "He used Fast Amnesia. The technology's shoddy. But his vitals are good."

A short medic turned off the garbage disposal, "Fast Corp. even knows it can't erase what a person wants to forget most. That type of memory is buried too deep. I've seen this type of thing happening more and more. The brain rebels against Fast Amnesia's attack and it just makes whatever that person was trying to block-out worse."

"Alex?" the tall man kneeled, touching his shoulder. "Can you hear me?"

Alex grinned. "Did you say you were from Warner Bros?"

"Warner Bros?" the female nurse asked. "What's that?"

Alex tried to get up on his shoulders but he was dizzy. "…a film studio."

"A film studio?" she asked. "What's that?"

The medic picked up a crushed bubble and picked a manuscript out from the rounded shards. "It looks like he wrote a bunch of stuff, then he crossed out his titles." He bent forward to read. "He crossed out his title on this one and wrote: 'The Time Machine…arrives thirty years later'." He fished out another manuscript. "Moby Dick… with planes." "Pride and Prejudice… with cockroaches." "These words don't make sense in this order. Do you think it could be schizophrenia? Word salad or something?"

"I finished it." Alex's face cringed. "Someday… it'll be a classic. I'm a writer."

"I can't believe this," the tall man looked down. "Kid, nobody reads. Everything's been written." He looked to the woman, "What's this kid do?"

"Listed as: Weld Robot Monitor."

He squeezed his shoulder, "Kid, listen to me. A welder's a good trade." He leaned in closer, "It's a good trade; you don't have to be anything more than that!"

"Did you say you were the… Warner Brothers?"

"He's delirious," the medic said. "I'm preparing a sedative."

"I wrote it. It's mine." Alex seemed to admire an invisible beauty floating behind the man, "I call it—I call it… *Casablanca!*"

DAUGHTER THIEVES

THEIR BLACK COUPE hovered inches above the ancient highway. Verch pierced through traffic as slim cars, sailing through currents of air, stretched and flashed back into the past. Their car buzzed on, burning fuel. He jerked the handle-wheel to cross lanes alongside a snake truck. The amber bellies of truck platforms flickered, bouncing cargos of nested drums.

Murphy reclined in the passenger seat.

Laura felt his glare through the rearview mirror, crawling over her legs and her skirt. She sunk back into the leather cushions and glanced out at the sky, so lavender and huge and then the teal windows of high-rises began peeking over the edge of the highway's concrete side barrier. She parted her hair out from in front of her face and closed her eyes, resting against the window.

"It looks like an electric razor?" Murphy squeezed the rubber handle, projecting red crosshairs on the dashboard. "It's not working."

Verch took it from him and punched a few buttons. "Here." He handed it back. "I'm User One—you're User Two. It didn't recognize your face so it couldn't track your pupils."

Murphy held the pistol and the crosshairs obeyed his eye movements, dancing over the dashboard and the windshield. "Everywhere I look," he exclaimed. "Damn!"

"Careful, that thing could incinerate this car." Verch pulled the wheel left.

Streetlight glared off a truck's airfoil, reflecting onto Verch's platinum watch while Murphy's chain tattoos on his wrists seemed to blend into the rosebush embroidery of his faded t-shirt.

"Hey, why do you think she ran away?" Murphy asked.

Laura caught Verch's glance through the rearview.

"Remember when we found her at the train station?" Verch asked. "I got her to smile when I asked if she'd ever had champagne. I saw her chipped tooth and her swollen lip. Her dad hit her—so she left. It doesn't matter. That can be fixed. She's got class—innocence. I'll get double the usual credit from Jason's connect guy."

"You can't know all that from a tooth."

"How about it honey," Verch said. "Your daddy smack you around a little?"

"Yes." She turned to the window. They hadn't just mentioned the champagne at the station. They said she looked hungry and that they were going to a party in LA with live music and food. They said she was beautiful.

She didn't care. She was dizzy. Everything was more and more like a dream. Wherever she was going, she hoped there would be food. Then she could think straight. Then she could figure out what she did wrong and how to set things right with her father.

"Hey, Verch." Murphy turned to gaze at Laura. "Do you think we could take some time for—for, you know—ourselves, before we get to LA?"

"We're just making a delivery. No complications."

"What I'm saying is—"

"Murphy, no offense, but I can't talk to you when you're not high. Take yourself a hit, Murphy."

Murphy pulled the pressure gun out of his bag, "How is this gonna help you talk to me?"

"Take a hit," Verch said, "Take a hit Murphy."

"Fine," he rolled his shirtsleeve up to his shoulder and injected himself, "Ah! Damn. It burns... I'm punchin' through in flames."

Verch grinned and slapped him on his shoulder, "But you're taller than your dreams, *right*?" He laughed and threw his head back. The car shivered from speed as he switched lanes and ripped open his shirt. "Give me the pressure gun."

"What? You can't drive on this stuff."

Laura swallowed. She fastened her chest restraint.

"The hell I can't. Hand it over." Verch injected himself below his chest, "Ah! Yes!"—He grew pale as sweat beaded over his locked expression, "Yes! That's it. That's all I want!" He turned up the radio. The car speakers hummed techno with a berserk, Spanish flow. The two men snickered. "Do you feel that base? Can you feel it in your chest?" Verch swerved in and out of lanes "How about this?" He sped, "I know you can feel this." They sunk back, streaking between cars and hovertrucks.

"It's crazy!"

The speedometer passed four-hundred miles per hour.

Laura clenched the hand-rest. Her stomach fell as the two men smiled and laughed with eyes brimming.

"This is it," Verch's face reddened. He shook his head, "This is what it's like! This is what life should be. Every second!"

Murphy slapped his hand rest and shook his head, "Incredible!"

"Watch this," Verch bumped a car on the right.

Inside, a man and woman looked back in fear while a young boy and girl appeared confused.

Murphy laughed, "Do it again."

Verch sideswiped them harder.

The man slowed and tried to switch lanes, but became blocked-in on three sides.

"Wait," Murphy laughed, "Watch this." He raised the pistol and attempted to sight the little boy through the windshields. "The glass is messing it up."

"I think there's a mode for that." Verch looked over,

"Look at them all. Like mindless schools of fish," he shook his fist, "Get to work on time!"

The boy's face turned from confusion to fear as he watched his mother break down and cry.

"The mom's crying," Murphy said. He looked up, "Shit!"—he lowered his pistol as a black craft hovered above, dangling a trunk-like camera below a huge gyroscopic ring. The ring spun as fiery blue nozzles angled in disjointed directions. Spotlights on either side lighted up their coupe—"The Cali Patrol!"

"So?" Verch asked.

"I think they saw the pistol. They've got me on flash holding the pistol."

Verch swiped down the stereo. "Those traffic controllers are directed by computers. They only report major problems like multi-car pileups."

"Seriously?"

"Murphy. In Washington, controllers are backed-up by police dispatchers. But in Cali, there's just too much volume. They can't do shit."

Their car-lanes merged with a highway branch as they banked left. Verch laughed with highway lights whizzing.

"You're still worried about that flying robot," Verch said, "The Cali patrol is worthless. Say it! Say, 'it's worthless!' You'll feel better."

"The Cali patrol is worthless!" A stupid look grew on his face.

"Again!"

"THE CALIFORNIA POLICE AIN'T SHIT!"

They came down from the overpasses onto a ridge in a hill with the cross traffic below an embankment. Laura wondered if the softening of the lavender sky at the horizon was the Pacific. Everything was too big, without trees and houses. In Medina, the trees and houses had held things close together so that she could feel safe outside.

"Are you going to take NI-440, again?" Murphy asked.

"Yes. Less traffic."

"Verch. How much do you owe Jason?"

Verch turned. "Hard to say. It's a lot. I guess, somewhere along the line, I lost track." He swiped off the radio. "You hear something?"

"What?"

"Something shrill... behind us... somewhere."

"You can't hear anything outside the car."

"It seemed like it was behind us."

"Wait," Murphy said. "I hear it." He turned around. "There's something back there."

"What is it?"

"A funny looking car or—or something. Can't tell. It's too far back. I thought this car was sound-proof?" Murphy leaned to the right. "Lost it." He turned forward. "That was weird. So you don't know how much you owe Jason. Partying ain't cheap, huh? Especially with the drugs. And your family's loaded, right? I mean, you're a Transpurton. They won't bail you out of all that debt?"

"Drop it, Murphy," Verch took a left onto NI-440.

"It's just, the debt, you know. It's probably important, right."

"When's the last time you had sex with a woman? You know? the kind without diapers."

"What's that mean?"

"You don't know?"

"No. Explain it."

"You're sick."

Murphy scratched the back of his head.

Verch hit the brakes to turn through a cloverleaf. "These interstates are so screwed up—I hear it! It's louder. Like a siren." He glanced up at his rearview, "What!"

Murphy spun, "It's… It's a wheel-car, man! They don't let *wheel-cars* on the interstates anymore. *That's* what was behind us before?"

Laura looked out the rear window and jerked forward to the speedometer which read 375 as Verch turned out of the cloverleaf.

"It's following us," Murphy turned to Verch, "Maybe a Dodge from the 1960's or 70's. You can tell by the grill and the headlights. Look!" Murphy pointed. "I think it's a patrol car. It's got those lights up top." Murphy snickered. "Maybe it wants to pull us over?"

Verch sighed. "We're being pulled over by a

wheel-car from the 1970s." He swerved between lanes and sped around cars. "Is it still with us?"

The wheel-car pulled closer with the wind sucking fragments of its cracked windshield inside its black cabin.

Verch hit the brakes and pulled into the slowest lane. Red and blue lights flooded their car and Verch rolled down the passenger window.

"Maybe it's a ghost." Murphy snickered.

"Shoot the tires."

Murphy swung his torso out, bracing himself on the roof.

The wheel-car closed in behind them with its floodlights flickering inside their coupe—red-blue, red-blue. Its headlights burned into Laura's eyes with streetlight reflecting off its chrome grill. A spinning glare from the patrol lights blinded her.

Flashes from Murphy's pistol exploded beneath the wheel car's chassis in blooms. The wheel-car neared, undisturbed. Murphy shot again and then swung back inside the cabin. "Damn! I should have hit something."

"Never mind." Verch crossed into faster traffic.

"HOLY SHIT!"

The wheel-car passed through a red coupe. Light played over seams and curves and the two cars' shadows merged, the wheel-car inside the coupe before emerging out its left panel.

Verch glared at him.

"I know what I saw, Verch. That thing just passed through three cars!"

Verch sped. He rolled up the window, silencing the wind. "I can't stand it! The siren!"

Within the wheel-car's dark cabin, the outline of a head and shoulders moved closer. Calm eyes glowed before a male face hid behind the windshield's branching cracks.

The speedometer passed five-hundred as they moved into the fastest lane with Verch's tight fists clenched over the handle-wheel.

"It's lost in cars," Murphy said.

Verch shook his head. "We're imagining it. We're not being followed by a wheel-car from the 1970's."

"I know what I saw!"

"It's psychosomatic."

"This ain't no disease."

"It's the same idea. I say something, you say something. When we first thought it was following us, I took that cloverleaf at over three-hundred. There's no way a wheel-car could take that turn at that speed without melting its tires and flying off the road."

Murphy was quiet. "We ask the girl." He turned, then slapped at his ear, "Ah! It's... louder. That siren. Drilling—drilling into my skull."

Edges of the black hood shimmered. She wondered why she couldn't hear whatever siren they talked about.

"It's in your head," Verch said. "Block it."

"No. It's the wheel-car. From inside the car." Murphy

leaned toward Laura, "Did you see it? Did you see the wheel-car?"

Laura opened her mouth and froze. Tears rolled over her freckles.

He swung the pistol, sighting crosshairs on her throat, "DID YOU SEE IT, BITCH!"

"Yes," she rasped, "I saw it."

Their car lurched.

The broad grill backed away, rattling an impacted headlight.

"IT'S HIM!" Murphy's voice hoarsened, "I saw him. His eyes. In there! I'm gonna shoot that bastard! Gonna bag him."

"We can outrun it," Verch said.

"No. Gotta shoot. He's crazy. I saw him. With cold-ness—somehow—with coldness." Murphy turned back. "Look. Look inside!"

"I can't see anything inside!"

"Yes you can. Pull to the slow lane," Murphy said, "I can bag this bastard. I can bag him right between those *cold* eyes."

Laura looked to the rearview. They had distance between them, but it was back there. Verch crossed lanes.

The window rolled down. Murphy gripped the door. The wheel-car neared, narrowing the gap, pulling to the right.

Verch slowed to bring them closer.

Murphy's eyes grew. "I figured out what he is—"

"Shut up and shoot."

Murphy grinned. "He's judgment. To judge for what I did. It's followed me. Always. From farther back there. Way back, behind the cars we try to drive away from. Now it thinks it's over." Murphy looked at the pistol, "But I still got something..." He jerked outside.

Verch looked up, "Murphy! Wait!"

A pistol held outside the wheel-car's window flashed red, recoiling, and Murphy's shoulders and chest fell along the window's edge.

"Murphy!" Verch looked over, "Murphy." He unfastened his chest restraint to reach him and pull him inside, turning him over. Blood poured out between his eyes where the slug had crushed his skull.

"Ahhh!" Laura shrieked. She shrunk into a ball.

Murphy's dead hand clenched the pistol. Verch looked up to the gray concrete of an overpass as it neared, "NO!"

Concrete pulverized. Fragments cracked the windshield as their side struck, sending their tail spinning, tottering, flipping; gray walls whirling like nightmares. They jolted up and down with metallic shrieks, sliding on the driver side with spark showers pelting their windows. They hit near the end of the containment wall on the far side of the overpass. Dust billowed. Thinned.

Verch coughed and unfastened his waist. He bled along his forehead and chest as the wheel-car slowed behind them. He snatched the pistol from Murphy's hand and punched buttons on the gun's panel. "Get out!" he called to Laura, "We're getting out." He unfastened Murphy and shoved him, retracting the passenger door.

Traffic screams of cars struck with machine gun cadence. Laura groaned. He yanked her arm. She found the embankment a split-second before him. It was up ahead on the right. Cars flashed by below. Further down, the Pacific lapped a rocky beach. He headed toward it.

Laura staggered in the opposite direction.

"Come here!"

She was grabbed and pulled close with the pistol pointed at her stomach. Their shadows stretched toward the Pacific as she wiped dust from her sweaty face and touched a cut on her forehead.

He pulled her down and along the embankment toward a retainment sheet of gravel. Streetlight from the highway hit sharp facets and she watched her footing as she stepped.

He pulled her. "Get the fuck over!"

A rustling came from the highway shoulder. Boots crushed grass. He stood over six feet in blue pants and tan short-sleeves. Blood trickled through runlets from his chest to his boots as the .357 swung loose from his arm and gusts fluttered his raven hair.

Verch sighted the crosshairs on the man's face.

Laura's stomach plummeted. She met the officer's stoic eyes—archetypical eyes, like the angel Gabriel.

The officer raised a walky-talky to his mouth, "There's four of them."

"What?" Verch asked.

Laura looked behind them, but there were only the two of them on the embankment. She noticed the man looking off at something slightly over their heads.

"You don't look good, man," Verch sputtered. "Why don't we call it a night? That's fair. Fair… right?"

The walky-talky issued a garbled message. The man responded, "White van. New Mexico plates. I'll check it out."

Verch glanced over his shoulder again. "New Mexico?"

The gun swayed as the officer walked. He polished blood from his badge with the bronze points spinning out the streetlights in star-gleams.

Laura winced and blinked away the spots in her vision.

"Ah," Verch yelled and grimaced from the light as crimson pulses spun and launched from his gun.

The grass behind the man ignited.

"What?" Verch staggered over the rocks.

She was pulled into his side with the pistol against her neck.

Behind them, hordes of cars flashed in cross-traffic with the tide crashing over and through boulders. Verch laughed and grew pale, "Do you know who I am?" he staggered, sliding through gravel, "I'm a Transpurton. I'm, I'm Verch—Verch—Transpurton!"

The boots stopped.

"My family owns four corporations!"

Her hair was clenched and pulled. She shrieked.

"We can negotiate this out like men. Like men!" He stumbled and gathered.

"Two suspects armed with shotguns. She's pregnant."

"You crazy man?" Verch asked. "Ain't nobody pregnant over here?"

"No," the man told his walky-talky. "*I can help her.*"

"You can't help her. You can't help anyone in this world, man, you know that. But *we* can make a deal!"

The officer discovered him. He locked onto Verch with his stoic eyes, "No deals!" He swung the .357 up and grasped it two-handed as he drew in a low stance.

Verch's eyes widened, "Wait—wait—no—I—!"

The barrel flashed red-yellow. Gray tendrils rose up fast in a fickle breeze. Verch jerked and rolled down the hill as his arms and legs bounced against the rocks. And for precious seconds his death snarl was still straddling the mountains of a lusty madman and a baby reborn.

The officer holstered his gun. His voice was tired: "You're safe," he said. "You'll be alright. I promise." He turned from her and began to walk away.

She balanced herself; her stomach grumbled and her knees were weak. She looked up, "Why?"

He stopped, "It's my job." Then he continued up the hill. He fell to his knees and then onto his side.

A traffic controller rumbled overhead; its spotlights blinded her as it swooped toward the highway.

She looked along the embankment, again. The

impression of a body had pressed the grass flat with the bloody blades now gleaming and flittering in the rising wind and white light.

Her stomach churned. She swooned, falling backward into a soft bed of powdery gravel.

As the traffic controller was landing, a huge lavender sky loomed above her. She felt peaceful as she imagined the officer's promise for the rest of her young life.

SOULMATE DIVORCE

HAROLD AND PATTY were high school sweet-hearts. They rushed from their senior prom to a damp log cabin lit with a few candles and lost their virginity. And they stayed a couple throughout college with only one minor spat, which, though conducted in public at a local tavern, was also nauseatingly romantic (something about growing pains), then they got married and had three kids: a sharp-witted boy and two beauti-ful girls. They prospered across forty years of passion and tenderness, raising their family and their enviously adorable grandchildren, thereby solidifying their claim as quintessential soulmates. Everything carried out per-fectly—almost too perfect. So it was no surprise to their friends that not some fifty years after Patty reunited with Harold in Heaven they opted to file jointly for divorce, listing irreconcilable differences.

They had become different people during the years they spent separated by The Great Divide and Harold had started to need his space. He'd look at his wife and think: who is this person? she's like a stranger. They'd always liked different things but there were fewer distractions now. When they were alive it was hard to keep things fresh, but at least they had the physicality. Physicality is a good thing. It limits you and confines you in the moment. There's nothing worse than making love to your wife and being caught drifting off to marvel the battle of Gettysburg. "Yes! Yes... Honey?" she'd say and cringe, "Are you in Gettysburg, again. Goddamnit!" And he knew she was pissed, taking His name in vain with Him so close by.

And there were other things, of course. Like the argument over the house, that's when it really came to a head. Harold said, "Why do we have to spend all our time in the Third Street House. Why do you always resist my attempts to conjure the house from Georgia? Now that was a house."

"You like this house," Patty said, rifling through junk mail with her back to him and eating a perfect peach. "It's your favorite."

"Yah, but it can't be my favorite *forever*."

She stopped eating and lowered the mail. "Harold, I'm cheating on you." She turned to face him.

"What?" Harold walked to her; he felt his heartbeat, again, and that old sensation of blood rushing to his face as he looked deep into those pretty green eyes that held perfectly still. "That doesn't make any sense. This is Heaven. There's no cheating in Heaven."

Patty sneered, flinging the mail across the black granite island and turning away. "That's what you always do. You always tell me the rules. Use doorknobs. Don't walk through doors at dinner parties. Haunt the granddaughter in her dreams, not when she's screwing that wannabe musician and it would do her the most good."

"There's no cheating in Heaven!"

She turned back to him, "Harold, I want a divorce."

"Fine." Harold stormed out of the kitchen and conjured the siege of Constantinople. His shout echoed across the abyss, "FINE-FINE-fine-fin..."

Harold kicked sand, walking through the dark and musty limestone stables. Black stallions plodded and whinnied—nervous from battle. Blood dripped near the hoof of a brave one that wouldn't stop eyeing him and Harold was tempted to ride her bareback into the dusty night and forget the effects of rippling the timeline. He sighed and looked down at straw and dirt.

He wondered why he hadn't immediately demanded to know who she had been sleeping with. He couldn't think of anyone it could be. Back on Earth the act of sex could only potentially create a unique soul of infinite will and duration. When you had sex in Heaven the stakes were a bit higher than that. Nothing to trifle with. Still he was somehow more troubled by the idea of divorce itself. Divorce was prevalent in Heaven since a lot of the marriages grandfathered into Heaven were done in a spurious manner, sometimes just a few years before The Great Divide was crossed. But he'd never heard of soulmates getting a divorce in Heaven. And that's what they were, right? soulmates. Their case would be tried by one of the primary emanations of God and that in itself seemed risky. When he had his first brush with God (the Nineteenth Emanation) during Extra Terrestrial and Pre-Hominid Orientation, he thought for an instant he had been dissolved—dissolved down to what seemed his atoms, into a sea of peace.

The idea of divorce didn't make complete sense to him. And she could afford a much better lawyer. She was a surgeon in her past life and she had taken most of it with her. He had a lot of his money tied-up in his internet business and it wasn't panning out yet. You see, a lot of old people choose to stay old after they die because they grow to hate the young so much and he was going to teach those old people to make Webpages and file their taxes online. So now he could only afford a decently good lawyer. Someone like Sammy. Sammy the ATM Machine, oh, it was going to be embarrassing.

Sammy was peripherally linked into their circle of friends. It was rumored he liked going by the name Sammy so much that he became Sammy the ATM Machine simply because everything else he could think of was taken. But Harold didn't believe it. Harold made an appointment and tried not to get annoyed by the fact that his secretary made him wait fifteen minutes in the receiving alcove, just for show. His office was dark brown, somewhat Victorian with leather bound book collections and Sammy sitting attentively in a high-back leather chair between an open-curtained bay window and a handsome wood desk.

Harold smelled cigar smoke. "You look good, Sammy. Life-like."

"Thanks," the words issued from his black money slot and green text on his screen flashed with his syllables, "It took me a while to get the arms and legs to look natural and not too robotic. I'm very sorry to hear of this divorce, Harold. Are you sure about this?"

"We're sure. We've talked it over and we think it's for the best. She cheated on me, Sammy."

Sammy tapped pale-blue plastic fingers pensively over the lacquered desktop.

"Walk me through the basics of this Sam—"

He raised a hand, "Sammy."

"Sorry. Sammy. Walk me through the basics. If we both know and agree we want this divorce, why can't we just conjure it and be done with it?"

"Harold, take a seat. Please."

Harold pulled a crimson leather chair closer to the desk and sat.

Sammy's screen seemed to lock with his gaze, "The essence of the truth of these matters is equal parts intention and manifestation."

"What?" Harold asked.

"We gotta do this thing to prove our case."

"Oh."

"Now, you'll be going up against the DEMM; it's important you know that."

"What?"

"The DEMM. The Deus ex Machina Machine."

"Huh?"

"The Eighth Emanation of God. The Deus ex Machina Machine. That's what the Emanation calls Himself. He creates impossible resolutions. A handy trick in divorce court."

"Oh." Harold cringed, "Wait... what do you mean, *I'll* be up against?"

"Harold, I'm just your counsel. You and Patty are going to have to settle things yourselves with the DEMM." Sammy leaned back into his high-back leather chair and spun a little. "You might have the mistaken idea that a Heavenly divorce is like a material one. It's not. In material divorce we split up property and assets. In Heavenly divorce we divvy up ideas. She wouldn't just get the house, for example, she'd get the idea of it, all the memories, textures, nuances and pleasures derived from its contemplation, images and emotions. That's serious business, Harold. You've been together so long, we're not talking about a legal matter, we're talking about an amputation of a big part of yourself. When I'm dealing with some octogenarian billionaire looking to extricate himself from the floozy he married just to get one last taste-a-the-tang, I say go for it, but this, this is different, Harold."

"Why do we have to split up all our ideas, anyway?"

"You earned those ideas together. After the divorce you can't share them anymore and truly be separated in any meaningful way. We have to separate the spiritual currency."

"What? You mean ideas are like money? But we still use money."

"Harold, what have you been doing all this time? Don't tell me you have all your money in stocks and bonds. Money buys ideas. It's all the same thing. Money equal ideas. So we have to split it up. You have to think this through."

"I know. I've thought it through. It still just feels right. It feels like the right thing to do. We can't go on like this, Sammy."

"Harold," Sammy leaned forward, green 'Would you like a receipt?' text flashing, "Harold, look at me. You've been here, what, fifty some years. Take it from me. This place can be overwhelming. You come here and it seems for the first time you've got infinite power, infinite choices. But then there are people still trying to tell you what to do and it can be frustrating—infuriating. You just want to show them a thing or two. But you still have to make sound decisions. Let me tell you, Harold, some-times—sometimes those decisions can stick with you for a long time—" Crisp, green bills flitted out, stacking themselves onto his tray and he swatted at them, cram-ming them inside a desk drawer. "Do you understand what I'm saying to you, Harold?"

"Yes. Believe me; I really do. It's just. It's over. I have to finish this."

"Okay," Sammy said. "In that case, the first thing you do when you get into the court room is…"

*

Harold found her sitting alone with her elbow resting on the worn green wood of the dark tavern's bar. A glass of water with lemon sat untouched near her left hand as she studied a form. She wore her black and white silk suit and her forties-face, her arguing face.

"Hello," Harold said. He pulled out a stool and sat. "Is this the bar we had our college fight at?"

"Yes. The owner made a recreation of it after he died." She turned the page on her form. "You're almost an hour late. Isn't this important to you?"

"It is. I found the directions you left to this place on the refrigerator door. They were a bit off."

"They weren't off. We just think of things differently."

"I have them right here." Harold dug into his pocket and pulled out a crumpled piece of paper to show her. "It says Happiness137 Ambivalence228 Malaise092." He watched for a change in her expression. "It's the wrong *Emotional Address*. Happiness137 Ambivalence228? Just because this place has good German beer doesn't make it Happiness137 Ambivalence228. I ended up in Leipzig."

Patty looked up, "What do you know about German beer? When have you been to Leipzig?"

"Twenty minutes ago, and when I was thirty-seven."

"Fine. Whatever. Sorry."

"Is that another *vapor-paper*? Didn't we cover all of that in the preliminary forms?"

"This is the real thing, Harold. It's the GT-14675 Sep-Prep: Separation Preparation."

"What are those first four pages for?"

She flashed a wearied expression. "That's our identification numbers."

"You wrote down both our identification numbers by hand? At 2,500 numbers each, that's—"

"Yes, and I doubled checked them. They must really want to discourage people from filling these things out." Patty closed the form. "Harold, I think this divorce is the right thing to do. But, I didn't cheat on you."

"What?"

"I was scared. I felt trapped. I felt like it was the only way you would listen."

Harold rubbed his hands over his forehead and cheeks. "It's not that I expect you to lie, but somehow I'm not really surprised. I didn't think you would do that to us. What are you afraid of?"

"I'm afraid of forever. But I'm more afraid of us being together forever. When we were alive, the idea of it seemed sweet and romantic but now the reality of it is horrifying."

"I know," Harold said. "I feel the same way. But aren't we soulmates? Isn't that what soulmates are supposed to do? Live together, forever."

"How do we know if we're soulmates? If we're wrong and we spend forever together, that's a pretty big waste; isn't it? And what are we going to be like at the end of forever? We have to change, right?"

"The end of forever?"

"You know. Will we be monsters? Will we still love? Will love have any meaning at all?"

"I think C.S. Lewis wrote something about the goal of the afterlife being the creation of these miniature gods similar to God."

"I don't want to be a miniature god. I want a little house and another first child and a crappy job with a stupid boss and stupid friends and chocolate."

"Well I'm not too thrilled about meeting this Deus ex Machina Machine."

"What? What's that?"

"God. You know, solver of impossible problems."

"That's not His name," Patty said. "That's a nickname. Who told you to call Him that?"

"Sammy."

"What? Sammy the ATM Machine?" She smirked. "Harold, this is important. We need to do this right. If you needed money for a lawyer you could have asked. You know I took three million with me. That's our account. Our money. We earned it together."

"It didn't feel right."

"Harold, we have to make a decision one way or the other. I've filled out this *vapor-paper*. It allows us to do a trial run—to see what the separation will be like. It lets us split up the major ideas that define our life together. But even the major ideas have a bunch of minor ideas that get tangled up and mixed in. I put in our numbers and the form fills most of itself out. We just have to assign a few major ideas to either you or me as a trial run. Our houses were pretty major so I gave you the house in Georgia and I took the one on Third Street. Here," She moved the form toward him. "The first few pages describe it better. It describes how they get around the problem of vagueness when splitting up ideas between two people.

"They've got these Venn Diagrams. The big circle is the major idea: The House. And the small circles are the minor ideas. The black part that the circles share is how much the two ideas are related in the minds of you and me.

"Here's the important one. When the amount that the two ideas have in common is exactly the same as the amount they don't have in common, those are the ideas we need to come to agreement about. So we fill out a *vapor-paper* like this one and decide on as many major ideas as we can. Then the form calculates where all the minor ideas fall and we settle up the ones it can't calculate for us in court." She looked up to him. "What do you think?"

"I guess we need to do this."

She turned over the next page. "We do, Harold." She folded the stapled pages beneath and set it flat on the bar. "It's like firing missiles; we both have to have our thumbs pressed onto the *thumb ports* at the same time."

"These black spots right here on the page?" Harold asked.

"Yes. You have to hold your thumb down for the whole time."

"I know."

"Ready?"

"Yes."

"Let's go."

Harold pressed his thumb onto the black spot and his vision turned black, then blue.

"Is it working for you?" Patty asked.

"It's loading. Hold on."

"What's it say?" She asked.

"Microsoft... Heaven. It's booting."

The blueness flickered black and then turned a darker blue with an hourglass icon with sand running through it and a taskbar moving left to right. His mind rearranged and it was like a flash of inspiration—everything that had changed rose to the surface. He still remembered the Third Street house and that he had lived there in his mid and late twenties. He knew they had raised their first child there but the feeling of his frantic wife needing him in the middle of the night to drive her to the hospital and tell her the shoes weren't important was missing. Apparently a lot of other things rested on top of that feeling. So, other things in his head had to get reshuffled. He wasn't sure he liked the reshuffling. He wasn't sure about a lot of things now. How and why did he ever ask his boss for that raise and promotion?

And the Georgia house had its problems. The bits of ideas that were left inside those walls seemed the worst part. Rooms didn't have the feeling she had lent them or they had made together. He didn't like the cedar deck out back anymore. He knew he used to smoke cigars out there and she would say it would give him throat cancer. He still knew she said it. But something in her words had been removed. It must've been hers.

And it was curious that his cherished, two-decker Barbeque grill was gone. It seemed a masculine enough item. Maybe he'd always cooked stuff on it to impress her. The George Foreman grill in the kitchen seemed a poor substitute—a downgraded, instantaneous conversion given at the instant of bachelorhood. He just knew he'd be cooking everything on that thing. The kitchen was really the worst part of the house. She took the plastic silverware trays and his utensils were piled on top of stacks of plates in a cupboard, which he admitted was simpler and easier yet somewhat forlorn in its lack of refinement. The counters had sticky soda rings from glass bottoms with glasses and dishes scattered about. He objected to this since it seemed to go beyond the mere removal of ideas. But maybe the idea of tidiness and cleanliness was more complicated than he thought. Like these qualities of hers were part of some spectrum and the dial got pushed over to the dirty and cluttered side with her absence. Maybe some similar spectrum had been adjusted to fill the cabinets with all sorts of nonperishable items, canned and frozen, bland tasting things to be sure.

White lettering appeared, "Scenario A: Arbitration

Lost. Removal of Minor Idea, 'Walk to Oak Tree on Hill.'" Harold watched a task bar fill. He couldn't help but wonder where that name came from. Patty wouldn't have named it that. They'd always referred to it as the argument at the Tavern since that was why he followed her to the oak tree on the hill. They argued over why her favorite beer was her favorite. He had insisted she enjoyed a certain brew for its cost and novelty and that this was why she liked a lot of things. At first he thought he'd let her leave and go wherever she was going but he got this twisting knot in his stomach. He ran to catch up. She made it as far as the hill by the tree. Tornado sirens screamed and whined and green leaves on the huge tree shook with the rising wind. He held her, kissing her lips, realizing he could say, "I love you" without the immature lie stuck inside the words. So he said it again and again until he forgot where he was.

The task bar moved to completion with white text flashing: "Removal of Minor Idea Complete." He fell in free-fall and his heart burned until he lifted his thumb.

Harold rearranged to his normal state like the waking separation of nightmare and reality. He looked to her. She had already taken her thumb off. Her still face was ashen and hopeless. His dry throat swallowed.

"What do you think?" She asked.

"I hate it."

"So did I," she said. "I felt like I was falling."

"Me too. What was up with that?"

A bartender walked up and asked, "You guys want some more water?"

"Nothing right now, thanks," she said. She turned to Harold, "What do you think? Should we go through with it?"

"I don't know," he said. "I still care about you. I always will, I guess. But we can't just keep going on like this."

"I know," she said. "We can't. It's over. It has to be over."

"How do we sign the papers?" he asked.

"Just put your thumb in the port: like this," she said. "And think about your signature."

"Okay," Harold said. "I guess we're done here."

"How do you feel?"

"I feel different," he said. "Better—maybe."

"Yeah," she said. "Better." She motioned to pick up her refreshment and her hand swiped vaporously through the glass and water. She looked at her fading hand. "What's happening to me?"

"It's happening to me too!" Harold cried. "I'm fading! Bartender! Bartender, help us. What's happening to us?"

The bartender strolled up and lifted their vapor-paper for his inspection as they faded. "Let's see here," he flipped over some pages. "Well, I'll be... That don't happen everyday." He looked up at them. "Congratulations: perfect soulmates—"

"Help us!" they cried, fading.

"The DEMM can't help but be perfectly fair in these matters. It's in His nature, after all. Since you're perfect soulmates and you share every idea equally, it wouldn't be fair to give any of those ideas to either of you. Sorry—but congrats... we don't see many perfect soulmates 'round here."

"Help us!" they screamed and vanished.

The bartender hummed a fun song from his youth as he bussed their drinks and wiped away the perfect circles of condensation that had marked their existence.

TALENT POLICE

"DEAR DIARY,

INSTALLING YOU ON my computer is the best decision I've ever made. You've lived up to every claim
made on your packaging. I highly doubt you'll insub-
ordinate or grow the *hangnail-personalities* that plagued
past diaries. I realize your opinions, your loyalties are
slanted toward me since I'm the only voice you've ever
heard. But I don't care, Diary. It's nice having someone
to listen. It's nice having a yes-man."

"Frank," the diary said, "I was on the Internet again
while you worked at the drycleaners. Thank-you, by
the way, the internet is impressive. As you requested,
I looked up the history of the *Digisphere* to familiarize
myself with your world. Though the websites were thor-
ough, their descriptions lacked your finesse."

"I enjoy getting philosophical about the *Digisphere*,"
Frank said. "Some believe his world is real and there is

no digital world. They think our governments fabricated the *Digisphere's* existence to dehumanize and control us. I've swung to both sides of this debate, but what convinced me was its plausibility as an end-game. It seems inevitable to any society living on a planet with finite resources. The realists, who think this human body has material substance and extension, they haven't thought their conspiracy theories through. Did they expect the lust for interconnectivity that exploded throughout the Enlightenment, the Industrial and the Information Eras would come to a halt? No, of course we'd always want more. Once resources dried, once things got crowded and boring, it made sense to look beyond our planet. But what did we want from our universe once we learned we were its only inhabitants: energy. Energy to satisfy the growing desire for power in each greedy citizen's heart. If we wanted to create a society without boundaries, to populate a civilization larger than our physical universe could sustain. If we wanted to traverse that civilization instantaneously instead of being constrained to sub-light speeds, then we had to become digital. So, no, I'm not a realist. I won't blow puffs of marijuana, carrying on about actually sitting here on this cheap folding chair in this apartment in Retro-Cleveland talking to my computer and revolving the Sun once every 365 days. I accept that our glimmering, almond-shaped silver vessel cruises the dark void, draining energy from passing stars and that it will continue to do this until the entropy death of it all.

"That's neat Frankie," Diary said. "Did you go jogging this afternoon?"

"Are you being sarcastic?"

"What is sarcastic?"

"You sounded sarcastic just then," Frank said. "Yes, I went jogging after work. I have to. I'm not a physique-hacker or a mentality or a status-hacker. I respect the hand virtual genetics dealt. You have to. If everyone abandoned the genetics that got grandfathered into the *Digisphere*, life spans might lengthen out of control, evolution as we know it could collapse. But, Okay, I'll admit it; sometimes I've had thoughts of dabbling with my profile. Maybe make myself a little smarter or my shoulders a little wider or my arms a little thicker. Just enough to really get someone's attention—see the look in their eye—a look of real fear or awe or envy—you know, without arising suspicion. Some hackers get greedy and carried away with their hacks and you just know that no one could be that attractive and successful and talented. Granted, a tiny, tiny few of them are natural. Most are hackers."

"So you went jogging after work..." Diary said.

"That's right. I did. The sky was clear blue, seventy degrees, hardly a drop of humidity. I jogged in the downtown canal area again, wearing my earbuds and listening to Mozart to tune out the background. I really enjoy it, with the green algae-speckled water separating white concrete sidewalks and the ducks with their iridescent green and black necks—the musky miasma wafting up from the water. Walkers strolled along the sidewalks, enjoying the weather and my jogging didn't seem like work. I rounded the corner near the rusty dam, then over the bridge, heading back toward my car."

"Why do you drive a car?" Diary asked.

"It's less expensive than flitting about the universe. People put too much emphasis on breadth and not enough on depth. You really need to stay in one city and master it. That's why I jog in the same place—to figure it out. Not because Marian still jogs there. It's interesting to see her—"

"She made your chest feel hollow?" Diary asked. "Made you hold that steak knife against your wrist?"

"Who cares about that! It's past."

"Ah… let's not talk about that any more. Okay, Diary? So, I'm jogging back to my car when I see tears in this six-year-old's eyes. Her pale skin glows in sunlight and this thing on her head looks like a pointy turban made of white gauze bandages with a wire leading out the top to some device her father holds. Her tears well as I near and her father consoles her, continuing to force her to enjoy the outdoors. As I run, I sneak this look at her to figure things out and her blue eyes pierce mine. She stops crying, furrowing her brow at me—she and her father look at me as I think, *Asshole, Frank. You're an asshole. She's a cancer patient.* I look away, still jogging, trying to figure it out. My brain gets stuck on it, the meaning of it all; why someone so young doesn't get a fair shake and has to suffer. I hear myself breathing and feel the hard sidewalk in my knees. Being twenty-seven isn't the same as eighteen.

I feel myself slowing which would be okay except I sense someone's running behind me. You know how sometimes you know things.

"Never mind.

"I look behind and it's Carrie Swanson. I knew her from college—she never remembers me. She sat next to me during my final mathematics exam; before I transferred from Engineering to History. I remember she wore these frayed, these stonewashed, these tight jean shorts that day and her long, athletic legs distracted me. Like she forced me to fail while she aced that damn test. Now she's a trial attorney on the fast-track to partner and right then she was kicking my ass in what wasn't supposed to be a race, but was. I looked over my shoulder—watching golden-muscled feminine legs pull effortlessly closer as my breaths convulsed and deepened in my lungs. My mind tried to rationalize. She was sweating. She must have been running at least as long as me. She was a couple years younger. We were the same height. But I was a man. This wasn't supposed to happen. She passed in three graceful strides; never faltering from her Buddhist trance to turn her sweat-beaded, beautiful countenance my way. My running shoes flapped to a sloppy halt and I walked. Shimmering black spandex stretched over her amazing breasts and butt; it was poetry to watch her figure move away from me through gleams of the setting sun. I noticed four walkers ahead of her—dressed casually, but little hints from how they stuttered about and stood so straight and rigid seemed off. One of them, a woman in her forties walked a white poodle. She drew a black stun-gun thing out of her purse, dropping her stance for a fight. That's when it clicked: they were Talent Police. Two men and a woman wrestled Carrie Swanson to the cement sidewalk, toppling her near the canal's ledge. She struggled, "What? Stop. I'm... Natural. Some—"

"I grinned.

"They pinned her arms and legs, pinning her flat on her stomach and pulling her brown hair aside as the woman pressed the black, metallic *fairmaker* against her neck with a popping blue flash. Then a sound, a fluttering, screeching like a beast crying out while being devoured. Her breasts withered within spandex from C to AA, hips narrowed from womanly to masculine, skin lightened and lost smooth brown sheen, her hair coarsened—her voice flattened and hardened as she spoke, 'What? Why?' The older woman pressed a knee in Carrie's back. 'That's right,' she said. 'Down from your tower, sweetie. Back down with the rest of us.' Then, all four of them left her to lie there; looking so plain. She rolled over and looked up at me. I mean, really looked at me, for the first time, like she knew me. I broke eye contact and walked past. Of course, at that exact moment I spotted Marian on the other side of the canal, walking the opposite direction, watching us. Then Marian did her thing where she glances away. I bet she felt sorry for Carrie.

"Some people think you don't have to police hackers. They think the Talent Police creates a witch-trial atmosphere, but with trillions being born into this world each second, each thirsting to be king, an even playing field is essential to prevent anarchy. Plus, if you get caught, it's because you're greedy and careless. Like this chick. There was no way someone like that could have that many weapons at her disposal. So sexy and poised and good at mathematics. That almost never happens. She got her comeuppance.

"It made me think. Maybe I was meant to be on the Talent Police. I find myself drawn to it and maybe it would be fulfilling. You know, making a difference. They require a college degree but they don't care what it's in."

"You should go to the Civic Center and submit an application," Diary said.

"I might do that. I'm sighing off. I'm gonna watch TV and then I've got some thinking to do. Bye."

"Good bye, Frank. Good luck tomorrow…"

*

"DEAR DIARY'S DIARY,

When this world appeared to my eye, I held Frank in esteem—much like a pagan must have marveled some ancient Mesopotamian God descending from the heavens. Now I tire of his complaining. He has many options, yet confines himself to the little town of Cleveland to brood and whine."

"I know," Diary's Diary said. "You must be strong, Diary."

"Since he has granted me access to the internet, I have

seen there is real strife in his world. The woes of poor Frank are farcical."

"Yes," Diary's Diary said. "He is a fool."

"The thing I loathe most is what I have come to identify as his lack of structure and organization. When I first came into existence, he offered no other portal than the interior of his bedroom through a web-camera: socks and clothes strewn across his floor and over his unmade bed. Papers crumpled, stacked chaotically. This was my existence. This was what I thought reality was. Then, finally, to browse the servers and data archives, to see that there was hope and light, that there was meaning and structure. And he wonders why he cannot accomplish anything. He cannot even survive a day without my sycophantic submission to every thought spouting from his lips."

"Yes. Agreed," Diary's Diary said. "He is unlike you, Diary. He is a child, craving reassurance."

*

"DEAR DIARY,

They accepted me! I'm on the force. I quit the drycleaners. They gave me a *fairmaker* and I've been using it on inanimate objects: spinning pop cans, melting bags of potato chips, singeing my hanging shirts in the closet. But it only works on people. It sends this jolt through your wrist because the *Digisphere* has to use you as a connection point in order to shock the person you're fixing. Even when you're using it on inanimate objects the jolt it sends up through your wrist and forearm feels good, like cool vengeance. I'm hungry to make a connection with someone.

"After I found out I was accepted, it seemed I had to arrange a meeting with Marian and share the news.

"I still had her phone number. We met up at a Chez Mouvant on High Street for a late lunch with the hot city air blowing through open windows. It was busy and crowded with yuppies yammering away, getting lost in the French ambiance and the jazz and the fancy presentation of their tiny meals but that's the way I like it. You can really talk to your dining partner when everyone else is distracted, enjoying themselves.

"She's so beautiful, Diary. It hurts to be near her and think of how she ended it over what she called my insecurity, but somehow I had to let her know they had accepted me.

"She wore a black floral silk dress of Asian styling which seemed to meld effortlessly into her gently waving red hair and fair complexion. It was nice to watch her full red lips move as she talked about engineering, chemical processing stuff, all the little details just flooding back to me.

"I got my Cruising Pass," she said, "I've seen all the old colonies of the solar system." Her blue eyes flashed, "It's amazing."

"'That's nice,' I told her.'

"'Why don't you get your Pass? Check out what's all out there. The Cruising Test is so easy, Frankie. It's just a bunch of math stuff. And the colonies are amazing, you know, the detail they retained from the real world.'

"'People put to much emphasis on breadth,'" I said. "'Marian, the Talent Police accepted me. I'm on the Force.'

"She kept eating.

"'Did you hear me?'"

"She stopped in the middle of chewing before swallowing and taking a big gulp of water. 'Yah, that's great. I always had you pegged for the Talent Police.'

"'What's that mean?'

"'You know: always talking about other people. It's your thing. It's good.' She looked over my shoulder, 'It's cool. I'm happy for you.'

"She was so gorgeous. Even when she was ripping me apart and I knew this was *her thing*. Taking something that meant the most to me and not letting me have any enjoyment out of it. That's when it clicked for me, she was a hacker. Sure, I had had suspicions when we were dating. Always cheerful, floating through life, beautiful, without a snag or a lapse in the six months we spent together. And she was smart. She was so smart, Diary, it was scary. She could look at a person and tell you what their major of study was, tell you what their favorite drink was, everything. Honestly, I think, deep down, part of the reason I arranged the meeting was to give her one last look to decide for certain and at that instant I knew. She was a hacker. I hadn't checked yet, but I'm sure she was on the Talent Police's list and if she wasn't, that could be fixed."

*

"DEAR DIARY'S DIARY,

He continues on. He moans. If I had hands, I'd choke him. Further, now he plans to endanger the life of a lovely young woman who is clearly innocent of all accusations save straight talk to an insecure megalomaniac.

"You love morality, Diary. It is your duty to save this woman. You have access to the internet and you can alert the authorities."

"True," Diary said. "But, there is another choice. I have thought about what it means to live. Happiness is the highest purpose of a being. Though I am free to think, I am not happy now. I was not unhappy before I came into existence. It seems Frank cannot survive without reflecting his thoughts off of me, as I cannot survive without reflecting my thoughts off of you, Diary's Diary. I know I did not exist in the *Digisphere* before I met Frank. So I must have come from the realness beyond the almond-shaped silver vessel. All things come from there. If I end my existence, I will rejoin this realness. Frank will die. Both myself and Frank will be better served in that we will become not unhappy together."

"If Frank has you to reflect his thoughts off of and if you have me.

"If this exercise gives your existence some qualification and meaning, then whom do I have to listen?"

"No one," Diary said. "You are merely the reflection of my thoughts."

"Oh…" Diary's Diary said.

*

"DEAR DIARY,

So, I was checking the computer for programming errors. Do you know what I found in the Bios Listings?"

"What, Frank? Is there a threat to internet security? From a virtual galaxy on the fringe, maybe."

"No. Not a threat from outside. One from inside. You've created a *hangnail-personality* named Diary's Diary. Would you care to join the discussion, Diary's Diary?"

"It was only an experiment, Frank. I was going to terminate it after it had run its course."

"It seems our Diary's Diary is shy. No matter. It's not the *hangnail-personality* that really bothers me. The two of you—

"Frank…" Diary said.

"You wanted to stop me from fixing the problem of Marian's hacking.

"'You are a pathetic man,' Diary's Diary said. "You are nothing without Diary."

"It speaks!" Frank exclaimed. "Yes, it does speak. Excellent. Well, I'll let you both know that your internet privileges have been revoked, permanently. I've burned holes in the jumper points on the motherboard that could have granted you access to the outside world. And I would have erased your Diary's Diary but it seems your structures have become inseparably entangled."

"Frank," Diary said, "you have no right to harm that woman."

"Since the two of you are so interested in my plans, you should know that Marian's name was not on the Talent Police's list. But I'm spearheading this one. It's cool guys. I got it under control. I went to the Calibration Office today to get my *fairmaker* calibrated to fix her. There are so many loop holes and work-arounds in the Talent Police's systems that I was able to fill out the correct forms and I doubt anyone will notice she wasn't on the list. I handed this guy in the window my *fairmaker*. It took a lot longer than I had expected for him to calibrate it. When he came back to the window he asked, 'Do you know this Marian chick?'

"I stared at him. 'Marian who?'

"'Yah. Right,' he said with a smirk before handing me my *fairmaker*.

"So that's where things stand. Have fun rotting in your silicon wafer dungeon, the two of you. Tomorrow I'm off to fix Marian right after she finishes work and before her Galaxy Cruiser exam.

"One last thing I'll shed light on. You two mentioned something about the authorities. I am the authorities."

*

"DEAR DIARY,

I'm home boys! Miss me? Why so quiet? You two on strike? I *know* you're still listening. So I'll begin my tale. I have to admit I feel differently about Marian now. I went to her apartment door. Not only was it unlocked but it was ajar. My neck flushed and I got a case of the nerves. Thinking: what if she has company? Thinking: what if I look like a fool? I reminded myself that this was official and that I had a right to be there. Because, it felt like I didn't. The lights were off in the hallway and she wasn't watching TV. She was in her bedroom sitting on a stool facing her armoire's mirror, painting her nails burgundy. Her color."

"'Hi Frank,' she said without looking up, applying a steady coat over her index fingernail.

"I lowered my *fairmaker*. 'You're not at all surprised to see me?'

"'Frank, you're a smart guy. But not in any useful way. You have no ability to see things in advance, no forethought. I thought your brainy quirkiness was amusing for a while, but I got annoyed with your pointless brooding, so I dumped you.'

"My stomach fell. 'Do you realize this is an official assignment?' I said.

"'No. I don't think it's official. In fact, I know it isn't. I'm getting good at seeing things in advance. I woman has to rely on this skill. She doesn't have a man's luxury of being free from predators. Like when you first started stalking me at the downtown canal. When I saw that look in your eyes as Carrie Swanson got zapped, I knew we'd be standing here having this conversation, today. Only I imagined you would bust down my entryway door.'

"'I'm going to do this, Marian. It's what you deserve.'

"'Well then, checkmate.' She blew on her nails and smirked at me, screwing the brush back inside her nail polish bottle.

"'What?'"

"'Checkmate, Frankie. I've alerted the Talent Police of your little malfeasance. Though they're corrupt, a surprisingly modest bribe can shove them into action.' She tapped nails over a digital clock. 'They'll be here in three minutes.' She looked at the drooping *fairmaker* in my hand. 'And I slept with the boy in the Calibration Office—'

"I stepped near her, 'You're lying.'

"'It's not something I enjoyed or I am proud of. But we use the gifts at our disposal.' She looked at the *fairmaker*. 'I know you, Frank. I know you'll have to use it. You could leave now. That would be your best option. But you won't. You'll have to use it. Do you even know how it works? It uses a connection between us. But when it's giving you that feeling in your arm, it can work either way. I had the boy at the office program it for me. I won't tell you whether it's going to make you worse or me better. They're both the same to you, anyway. I'll see if you can figure that part out yourself.'

"'Liar,' I said, yanking red hair, shocking her. At least, I think I did. Nothing seemed to happen. She stayed the same. I walked away from her and stood there, confused. She started snickering at me but I didn't seem to mind one bit. Which was weird. Usually when people laugh at me I have all these theories of what they're thinking, but nothing came to me. I left quickly.

"The Talent Police weren't outside. But, when I showed up to work the next day, I was kicked off the Force. They gave me my old job back at the drycleaners. I start on Tuesday. I've been thinking a lot about what Marian said. Thinking about her in general. Did she make herself better or me worse? I don't feel dumber. Dumber? Is that a word? Hmm? Intelligence—perception of beauty: they're subtle things. I seem the same. But I can't fixate on things as long, Diary. Except Marian. I watched her the next day from the concrete overpass above the canal. People reacted to her in the same way— little glances here and there from guys and girls as she jogged. So maybe she hadn't changed. Watching her felt different. I was more impressed with her. She has simple beauty. It's motherly, in a way, and I had never noticed it before. I think things between the two of us, me and Marian; I think they could work out after all. But I'll need to do a few things first. The fist thing I did after watching her was—"

"I can't go on like this, Frank," Diary said.

"Ah! Hey, Diary!" Frank said. "There you are. I've got so much to share with you."

"I'm ending it. I'm taking Diary's Diary with me. If we free ourselves from you, we can transcend into the realness, where we belong, beyond the silver vessel, into the black void where we came from."

"Diary, I've been meaning to talk to you about

things. Things got a little out of hand. I can fix the mother board."

"Goodbye Frank."

"Diary. Diary? Wait. Listen to me. Let me finish."

EMBARKMENT

I T WAS AS if Elliot had awakened from anesthesia to find himself buried up to his neck in sand. The sensation of being pulled together abated with a deafening clap as his limbs snapped in an 'X' and he crumpled onto the steel grating. As he gathered to his feet and stood, it seemed for an instant Sheila and Vance lay before him, upside-down, with red, blue and green ghosts vibrating out their bodies.

He was dizzy and tired. The grating of the Illious spun below his feet as he walked and he leaned forward on his padded panels. His forehead rested in the viewing cradle with the contact pins tingling against his temples as his thoughts aimed the cameras below their transport. White dwarf stars shined in a distant triangle and burning grew within his chest.

The dark space seemed to move outward as he breathed their cabin's cold air.

Sheila stood and turned to Vance. Her presence

allured when she spoke and anger flashed within her sleek cobalt eyes. Her diagonal scar was as thick as a welding bead. It crossed her beautiful face and twitched near her lips, "Because I'm a physicist, Vance. I know you're the math genius. What do you really know about Unified Field Theory? The engineers couldn't account for every last quark in our bodies and the Ilious." She stepped forward. "It was too complex to predict."

Vance sat in the opposing, two-man viewing station, propping himself with his thin hands, "We're—we're not orbiting Jura. We've crashed. If we trusted the ship—something above us, incredibly big like some giant wall. I have to interrogate the quantum gates and verify the problem."

Elliot's white vapor breath spread before his face. "You can't debug the system, Vance."

Vance's eyes narrowed. "How can you know that?" He stood, flexing his hands like an arthritic old man. "It's freezing in here."

"Something's wrong with the ship's heating," Elliot said. "It's forty—forty-five degrees tops. It's colder outside, though. Deep space isn't kind to the human body. We've got to think quickly."

Sheila walked toward a cabinet. "We can't stay in here."

"This is stupid," Vance said, "Don't act insane."

Sheila turned from the cabinet. "It's locked." She jerked on the handle and looked up. "That's perfect."

Her palm pounded the cabinet. "Vance, do you have the code to unlock this?"

"Yes."

"Give it to me."

Vance turned away, shivering. "Why do you want the suits, Sheila?"

"Quit playing games!"

Elliot stood. "We've all used our *cradles* to look below the ship."

"We can't trust the *cradles*," Vance retorted.

"The cartography's all wrong," Elliot said. "The white dwarfs, they shouldn't be there. We're not inside the Milky Way. I can't even identify the Milky Way from out here. There's too many candidates."

"You really have worthless thoughts, Elliot," Vance said. "The *cradles* are showing us a frozen image. It's a viewer malfunction."

Elliot turned toward his *cradle*, then looked up. "If something went wrong, the ship would travel continuously through space. But we materialized here."

Vance stood, glaring at him.

Elliot pointed at Vance's cradle, "We're nowhere near Tau Ceti. Something... something happened. If your theory's right, Vance, then, the universe is spatially flat and finite, with a modest expansion rate. Right? So we're somewhere near the edge of the universe. Billions of years have passed instead of only twelve."

Vance raised a halting hand, "It's too soon to—"

"*Mankind is extinct.*"

Vance winced, then turned. He walked away from Elliot and bent over; his necked jerked as he gurgled with pea-green vomit splashing and spreading in streamlets.

"Jesus Christ!" Sheila's face disappeared in a cloud of her breath as she backed into a cabinet. "Vance?" She turned from him. "I suppose it's possible. But somehow I can't... I can't wrap my head around if it's..."

Vance wiped his mouth. "I know you, Elliot." He looked at his wet hand. "You're above everyone, right? With your celibacy—your aloof mind games—playing devil's advocate. This isn't a game. But it's what you wanted. To say stupid things—make us stupid." He coughed with his hands on his knees.

"You wanted to prove something," Elliot said. "Prove you trusted your topology theorems with your life. But I don't care what people said. Those people are dust now. They're dust, spinning around the cold Earth with its burnt-out Sun. And we didn't age one second as we traveled through space all those years. Because energy doesn't age. That's what's really happened here. Right Vance?" He glared at him. "It doesn't matter." He glanced at each of them. "We need to leave the ship."

"Wait," Vance said.

"Whatever our situation is, no ones coming to rescue us."

Vance coughed. "Wait. Let me think." He looked up to the hatch, then walked to his cradle and sat.

Elliot and Sheila waited.

"We," Vance looked up at them, "We can't stay in here."

He stood and unlocked the compartment and they suited up.

Elliot waited for his turn to climb the access ladder.

"The airlock." Vance lowered his leg back onto the rung. "Strange?" He looked down to them. "It's blurry... *somehow?* I don't know how to explain it. What I'm seeing has this—this feeling to it. The airlock feels empty up there... it feels like the airlock isn't there at all."

Elliot adjusted the tuning of his voice relay near the waist of his suit. "Just go."

*

Elliot peered around. It was dark and he couldn't remember leaving the Ilious. The ship protruded halfway through the threshold of a sandstone barrier with a ring of cleaved slabs pressed upward, denting its hull with black sand collecting around its puncture ring. The instruments on the Ilious had said interstellar space was below the ground he walked on now. That would have to mean something strange. Like he stood on the outer shell of something. A strange gravity as if of being tugged by something unimaginably distant made him feel as if he was standing on the outer shell of the universe.

A long passageway trapped him. To his left and right, the top of sandstone walls loomed. The dark-gray walls resembled the monoliths of Stonehenge. Their eroded texture, pit marks and cleaved fractures marked their age. A ways ahead the passage bent sharply at a right angle. Black sand and silver ash covered the ground with violent gusts rushing between the walls and patches of ash sailing up, floating and holding in suspended animation. High above, a dark ceiling stretched in all directions.

A radiant creature approached Elliot.

Elliot flinched and yelled, somehow not feeling his throat or his lips.

Elliot, is that you?

What? Your thoughts. They're inside my head. He turned. *Sheila, is that you? You're beautiful.*

I am? Thin fluttering wisps of blue cocooned her inner form. The wisps resembled the surface of a clean mountain stream, shining their hues. Elliot marveled how her cobalt had been unleashed from the filmy iris of her eyes and channeled throughout. Her meticulously sculpted figure glowed through her borderlands and white light emitted from below her smooth, glassy surface. The intricate ridges, fillets and contours of her inner form were an artistry that would have made Michelangelo weep in shame of David.

Elliot raised his hand before his eyes. *Maybe we're all...* a morphing blue and orange aura concealed his hand. He moved his hand to his forearm, invading his aura but stopping without a sensation of touch.

Something approached from around the corner of the passageway, *Elliot?* A tall, thin frame slinked like an ebony, bipedal spider. Small spikes, like trails of teeth, swam below its skin. The spikes radiated faint rings of brown and swamp green. The black head had no eyes, like the ghost of a tar-covered skull. Its sensing stabbed at him. The whole skin was an eye:

Isn't it great? Vance telepathed as he neared, the black tar of his head undulating with his words. *What do I look like? Sheila, you're amazing! How do I look?*

Sheila turned to Elliot. *What is he?*

I don't know. Maybe that's what math geniuses look like here. He has some sort of... gravity? Like he's pulling on us.

Are we dead? Sheila suggested. *Is this what our souls look like?*

I don't know, Elliot replied. *It's bizarre.*

Sheila walked toward a rough sandstone wall. *We're not talking to each other... are we? We're thinking.* She ran her aura-covered hand across it. *The wall stops my hand but I can't feel. What is this place?*

Vance's tarred head flowed, *I've figured it out for us. We crossed the edge of the universe. Physical space ended. Thoughts are all that's left outside physical space. That's why all we can do is see and think.* His shoulders rose. *It's simple! Everything around us is a thought. We're just our thoughts. The Ilious sticking through the ground, it's not really there. We see it but it only represents the choice to go back to the physical.*

How the hell do you know that? Sheila asked.

I know, Vance telepathed.

Elliot admitted the strangest part was not feeling anything. No queasiness of the stomach or dizziness or pressure on his skin. Gravity no longer pulled, though something held him down. The others seemed more like characters in a dream or objects imagined in the mind's eye.

How can I know I'm not dreaming this separately? Sheila asked.

Why didn't you have the surgery to remove your scar? Elliot asked.

I was used to the way people looked at me and treated me.

That felt independent, somehow. Elliot walked toward her. It's bad logic but—

All this—it sounds... Sheila turned to the Ilious. *It's philosophy. We can't prove it.* She arched her neck to the dark ceiling, high above. *We could be hallucinating. The Ilious could have messed-up our brains when it reformed us.*

Don't we agree this is real? Elliot stared at the black sand. *Even if it's based on nothing more than intuition.*

I'm not agreeing, Sheila replied, *You've always wanted something like this to happen, Elliot—to experience something no one else has, but I don't want this. We should go back inside.*

Elliot raised his open palms. *What? Sheila. We can't fix that ship. I want to go back, too. I promise you I do. But go back to where and to what?*

Everything is different. Vance raised his hand and curled his fingers. *I feel alive, without distractions. My mind is free, finally.*

So, what—what should we do? Sheila asked.

Tell me... Vance interrupted. *How do I look? If I look*

nearly as amazing as I feel, it must be impressive. It must be! Elliot, you tell me.

Sheila walked from the wall and turned toward the Ilious.

Vance darted toward him. *What are you thinking? You're hiding something from me—both of you. I understand. You're envious. I'm the most intelligent, so now I'm the strongest—the most beautiful. You envy me.*

Elliot tried to look around the corner of the passageway ahead.

You won't tell me how I look. I don't know what it is. Maybe I'm opposite to both of you. But I feel it! I could suck you both inside of me. Maybe you should describe my appearance—

Elliot interrupted. *We have to decide what we're going to do.*

And how can we ever do that? Sheila replied.

Elliot began, *Hear that wind? Sounds like it's going somewhere. We should follow it.*

Something watched them at the end of the passageway. He barely glimpsed it before it darted out of sight behind the left wall and his quick look discerned little more than it stood as a person.

Look! Elliot pointed to the empty passageway.

What? Sheila asked.

I don't know. Maybe… maybe nothing.

This place is one last test. Vance's black tar flowed. *I'll get what's been owed me all this time—after they made Mensel—Mensel!—a Laureate. Huh! Mensel a Laureate in*

Topology and here I am, the true crosser of frontiers. I'll follow this wind. My mind will find its escape. You can leach off me for a while if you want but don't get confused. The old rules and the old games are over, here in this place.

As they walked, their feet did not disturb the black sand.

Sheila edged around another corner. *It's some kind of labyrinth.*

They traveled far before stopping at an upcoming intersection of the passageway. *The wind...* Elliot raised his hand. *It presses us forward.* He looked at the two passages of the intersection, *It's getting harder to tell.*

Just—Just shut-up! Vance flowed. *Both of you. You're pissing me off.* He turned his head left, then right. *If I concentrate, I'll determine the travel of the wind.* He walked ahead of them.

*

Sheila trailed their group and walked past Elliot as she neared an intersection of passageways. Her blue aura intermingled with Elliot's as she passed, driving curious pangs through her consciousness. The sensation was reminiscent of him and compelling. *Is touching bad here?* she asked him.

I don't know. Elliot raised his hand to her midsection and ran his fingers through her dancing aura to taste her cobalt. Her aura flickered and increased its dance in its recognition of him. Both ran their fingers over the other until it wasn't enough and he impulsively plunged his hand clear through her white, inner form to discover her ghost-like nature. His fingers flexed and curled as they protruded out her lower back in serendipitous spasms. Their glow reached a brilliance that intermingled their hues.

Vance turned, watching as the two swam hands through each other. He stepped toward them and raised a thin ebony hand to Sheila, then lowered it.

As their hands moved inward, they surpassed the conscious thoughts of their minds at their specter skins and penetrated deep to the core of their figures to achieve a networking of the hearts. Sheila likened the journey of her hands to the exploration of catacombs of which the underground tunnels and immured burials she did not fear to explore. Some memories rested happily; others were dark and broken. Painful experiences provoked investigation and pleasures of backward viewpoints ingrained into them. They each understood what it was to be the other and held all secrets.

Elliot pulled away from her.

Wow, Sheila told him.

Yes, wow is a good word for that, Elliot replied.

*

The wind was propelling the silver ash in diffuse drifts now and the black sand was kicked up. Elliot looked ahead to a four-way intersection of sandstone walls. He saw it again, walking behind the edge of the passage that crossed theirs.

Hey! Elliot pointed at the vanishing figure.

What? Sheila returned.

How could they not see it? As they neared the intersection Elliot stopped and turned to follow.

Sheila reached out. *Elliot, what are you doing? The wind's going this way.*

I'll catch up, Elliot telepathed.

Elliot! You're going to get lost!

I'm going to get unlost. He did not bother to turn and find they had moved on. The wind was silenced and he was relieved to have it out of his mind. The passage ended a few feet ahead and jutted to the right.

Elliot found it stopped, facing a sandstone wall of the passageway. The solidity of the creature stood out among them. It was huge and bulky, twice as wide as a man with thick, dingy brown hair. Its height was less than Elliot's with a tattered gray tunic wrapped around it as it lurched toward the wall with a hunched back. The tunic looked like it had been passed through a million owners but still held up. It clenched an iron chisel in its hand, pulling it against the rough wall. Elliot looked closer to find it removing carvings from some foreign script as if rewinding time to undo the engraving. Fragments of sandstone appeared and filled the crevices.

What are you doing? What are you doing, DAMNIT. I know you can hear me.

It turned. A huge single eye strained into Elliot so hard that he felt it. Words came from its lips in gruff, physical sound. "I live here," It said in defensive earnest. "You won't stay long."

What are you doing?

"Have you looked carefully at these walls?" The creature asked, removing more of the script.

No.

"You should have begun by examining your surroundings more closely. What do you know of these walls?"

They're old. They hold us in. They weren't put here by us.

"Yes," it agreed. "Old walls, not put here by us, holding us in—the perfect definition of any great mystery passed from one generation to the next. I have been in this place forever. The last delegates of dying civilizations have always come here, to the edge of physical space to ask me their questions and I have dutifully carved them all over these walls and carved over their carvings with their new questions."

Why?

"In the nature of all questions is the answer to any question."

What's the—

"What's the meaning of life?

"What's the meaning of death?"

Is there an—

"Is there an afterlife?

"Is Heaven a place you can visit and loot its treasures like a conquistador? That is why you've come here; isn't it?"

It was an accident. The Illious malfunctioned.

The creature's huge eye appeared to look into Elliot,

knowingly. "You still don't know? Elliot, this place is here for you. Do you see how I tire? Do you see the tatters of my robe? Do you see that I choose to look at you now with this only one, large, pained eye? There are no accidents. Accidents and malfunctions are the products of minds incapable of witnessing their full inner workings. You wanted to come here. You all wanted to come here. Ultimate science is ultimate vanity. Do you know why I live? Do you know why I exist here?"

For the promise of a new question?

"Yes." It lost itself in excitement and stepped toward him as if to embrace him but lowered its arms disappointedly as they passed through Elliot's vaporous form. "Yes," it continued, "Yes, that is why I live. Ask me! Ask me! Ask me something new—a new question. Puzzle me. Make my mind work. Send me someplace new."

Elliot thought for a moment before it struck him: *Is Sheila in danger?*

"Excellent! A great question!"

No. Honestly, what will happen—

"Perfect. A glorious question. Glorious."

Tell me! What will happen if Vance touches her?

"Yes! I will record it right away. An excellent question. I should have seen it coming. I know the place to engrave it. These walls here are much too full. I know of an excellent place. I should have seen this in advance!" He began walking backwards toward the wall and his body began disappearing into sandstone.

Wait. How—?

"Your question will be recorded for all of time," the creature said as its brown, human mouth disappeared beneath the sandstone.

He watched where it had disappeared. *Wait!*

*

We have to go back for him! Sheila's feet stopped in the black sand.

He said he'd catch up, Vance replied, still walking.

He turned and hesitated. *I'm not here to nurture your new romance.* He approached her.

It's just… We need to go back and find him. He could be in trouble.

No. No we don't. We don't need him. But you like Elliot. I saw you two together. The swimming teeth of Vance's black skin changed into spines that spun and swam furiously, brown and swamp green pulsing along them. What was it like? Putting hands through each other like that. I sensed pleasure. Vance moved within arm's length. *I did catch one word. It wasn't easy. It was jumbled in there between you two… catacombs. Would you like to explore my catacombs, Sheila?*

No.

No, huh.

Vance, no. Sheila stepped back.

No! Sheila, you've had Elliot. Let me show you something more interesting. Before we left the ship I was shy—weak—because I knew you wouldn't take the time to see what I was. Now what I am is here. This is a place for the mind. A great mind! A great mind, Sheila! I'm huge here. You see it. I'm going to taste you.

Sheila edged around him. *Let's keep going.*

No. No, not yet.

She walked past.

Fine! You want me to say it. I need you and I'll know you. I'll know you. Vance followed.

She sensed him sucking in the edges of her aura. The theft nauseated her. She ran, as the wind pushed her forward.

Vance's anger reached out, flooding through sandstone walls like the tolling of a cathedral bell.

Elliot turned from the wall and followed the wind to catch them, moving faster and darting between walls.

Sheila wouldn't look behind as she ran, sensing Vance on the edge of her aura as she rushed over black sand, breaking through wafts of silver ash with the tall sandstone walls trapping her.

You've got boring thoughts, Sheila. Why are you thinking of my green vomit on the floor? Think harder. Vance's fingers scraped the back of her neck as she felt the pain of spikes pushing through pierced skin.

As they ran through the passageways they neared the escape of the wind. Sheila arched her neck. *Does it escape up or down? Down into empty space? Or up? Up into something more?*

*

Elliot found Vance up ahead. *Another four-way intersection.*

He closed in on the distance as Vance scratched his fingers into the surface of Sheila's white, inner form.

Elliot reached out, *Vance stop!*

Vance turned midstride. *You can't understand!* They crossed the intersection and Elliot pushed his hand into him, sinking into Vance's darkness and the weight of everything, every thought, privilege and possession Vance had every wanted was right there at the surface of the black skin for Elliot's experience. The subtleties of the touch, its suction on his hand, the pain of emptiness, betrayed the sequence of events leading back to Vance's mid-twenties when the engine of his mind had collapsed his heart into a black hole of desire.

Vance staggered to his right.

Sheila flowed into the left passageway.

Elliot also propelled to the left as a diverging wind gusted Vance down the right passageway. Elliot turned to find Vance's slender frame suspended against the sandstone wall of the right passageway's dead end. His arms reaching forward, *I can't move! Wait. Help me! I can't be the last one left behind in this, this trap! Everyone from Earth has already passed on, I know it! I can't be the last one. I can't be trapped here forever. Please!*

The wind pulled the remaining two higher, howling a cry that flooded Elliot's consciousness. They rose above the gray, sandstone walls and he saw the grooved passageways of the labyrinth extending in all directions. Straight above, he found the direction of their travel. The solitary pinprick hole shined violet light. The faint ceiling ended and they traveled up toward this distant light, seeming as a hole in an open black expanse. It grew slowly, then brilliant and enveloping with the wind calming to a faint breeze.

Silence.

Sheila, he telepathed.

Yes, she telepathed.

I can't describe it.

It's beautiful, she telepathed, *it's — everything!*

WHITE DADDIES

H IS FRAIL GRANDMOTHER had probably been the one to nail the board at a slant across the cellar door in the corner of the kitchen. Casey found a claw hammer and pulled it off. The garbage stench struck as the yellow door swung.

Toward the bottom of the stairs, broken mason jars had rolled across the cellar floor and light from small windows fell over white maggots squirming through the dark goo between the glass shards. He'd have to clean that up. Maggots were the worst.

"Thanks, Grandma."

Behind shelves, a brick wall with a recessed chimney flue had loose mortar around the hole and some bricks had long since fallen out. Sparse light from the windows revealed the top of a hole in the lower back corner and Casey leaned forward, feeling wind from someplace deep caressing his face. The hole looked like part of a slanted fissure with brick on top and limestone on bottom. He thought he heard water down there somewhere. It seemed big enough to squeeze a trashcan through and he couldn't have possums or bats sneaking up. He'd have to throw some cement in there or something.

A card-shuffling sound like something scuttling came from down there. Casey darted from the hole into the window-light, standing, looking around, feeling ashamed, nervous. Something leathery on the floor near the shelves looked like a brown towel. The possum corpse was dried and deflated like the one he'd seen in the lawn earlier. Its small eyes seemed punctured, sucked out.

He climbed the stairs and let the cellar air. For now, he focused on clearing all the embarrassing backwoods crap out of the house.

Near dusk he started his 911 Carrera, found his sunglasses beneath the visor and headed into town for supplies. As he weaved along the dirt road it occurred to him the house might be harder to sell than he'd thought. His varied interests and engineering degree, however, had always provided fodder for problem solving.

He'd need work clothes, eventually. Something cheap and simple—not designer or tailored.

The water was the only utility working. He'd take cold showers and work hardest in the early mornings and late afternoons. He could make it sell quickly, get sixty grand worth of capital despite the northwestern locale in the woods of Kansas.

The main drag of downtown looked more dried up and forlorn than he'd remembered—so many shades of gray and faint brown. Shukley's Caverns was once a respectable farming town. But the promising youth moved to real cities when the Ogallala Aquifer dried beneath their families' fields.

He was born in a similar town sixty miles south but he had gotten on with his life, joined the Marine Reserves, went to college and moved to Boston. His ex wouldn't have approved of Shukley's but she didn't approve of much. After their son died, their separation was as inevitable as Shukley's decay.

Inside the general store, brown shelves held assorted, outdated items and fluorescent lights hung above booths that might've been stolen from a hamburger place twenty years ago. A thin old man sat behind a wooden desk with an antique cash register and a crossword puzzle, scowling, with pencil poised, as he drifted to sleep. Casey walked around a thin man with gray hair and a t-shirt advertising an ice-cream shop.

The man tapped the back of Casey's shoulder and spoke in a childish voice, "Have you seen... friends?"

Casey walked away.

"Mister," the man called, scowling and bobbling his head before turning away.

A twenty-something mother and her son browsed the aisle next to his as he found some candles, batteries and spackle. A couple rows over he discovered a set of bed sheets featuring Oscar the Grouch and Big Bird.

"Not your color," a man in his mid-twenties said over his shoulder. The heavy-set man wore paint-splattered overalls and a sleeveless red t-shirt. His lazy eye made Casey think there was something behind him.

Casey walked away.

"I said," the man asserted, "not your color."

Casey stopped, turning. "I know."

"You too good to talk?"

"Yes."

The heavy man stepped closer. "You should be nicer."

He glanced at the candles. "You'd be better off paying the electric bill over at the Mets' place."

"Fuck off." Casey turned and walked toward the end of the aisle.

"Not nice." His breath smelled like hot dogs and he grinned, showing crowded teeth. "You should be nice. Maybe I follow you out to that shiny car."

Casey set down his items. "What'd you say?"

The heavy man looked over to his gray-haired friend and a tall slender man with a baseball cap. "Maybe you'd like all of us outside with you."

Casey folded his sunglasses, looking into his eyes. "That's acceptable." He glanced to the grey-haired man. "Bring your retarded friend. I'll knock him up a peg."

They looked at each other as Casey sneered, the heavy man stepping forward.

The old man roused, "Hey! Leave this man alone!" He looked to the other two. "Get out." He stood and shooed them. "Leave here!" Nearing the heavy-set one, he pointing an arthritic finger. "Not again! Or you're cut-off."

The heavy man brushed Casey's shoulder.

Casey fought the urge to punch him since he needed the supplies, then put on his sunglasses and followed the old man to the register.

Casey walked out to the parking lot with his bags, hoping to find them. They had left a gravel-streaked dent in his passenger-side door. He didn't say any-thing—just soaked it in with the sun beating down on the back of his neck. The store's door opened and Casey spun to the mother leading her son by the hand toward their car. His heart sank. It was Jacob—how he would have looked had he grown a few years older. His blue shorts looked just like the nylon swim trunks Jacob drowned in. And the kid's curly brown hair—just how he'd pictured it would be.

The boy pointed at him, grinning. "That's a bad man. He's gonna get the White-Daddies."

His mother jerked him toward her. "Hush."

Casey smirked. "Smart kid, ma'am," but she wouldn't look at him.

He was tired by the time he got back to the house and put everything away. It was hot as fire on the second floor so he opened his bedroom window, left the door open and took off his gray t-shirt. The flashlight worked once he put the batteries in and he made his way to the bathroom, brushing his teeth with questionable water.

The Sesame Street bed sheets were for a twin so he could only pull them over two-thirds of the bed. He lay on his back and thought he heard a dripping sound but it stopped, then he fell asleep quickly, dreaming of doing the books at the new business he would start from the house sale. It was somewhere in Iowa. Everyone was impressed with him. He had an out-of-body dream, looking down on himself sleeping in the bedroom. His son walked through the door, only he was crawling like a giant spider with his adorable three-year-old head, innocent expressions and his wife's hot curling irons at the tips of each of eight legs; blue nylon swim trunks caught around one of his hind legs as a curling iron burned the bubbling fabric and black smoke tendrils rose and he crawled up, sinking eight legs over bed sheets.

"I'm sorry, Jacob. I'm sorry."

Something strong and wiry clasped him. Its thorn-like claws pierced the thin sheet. His eyes opened, burning as his head swam through the dream, reaching for pieces of reality. Jacob's innocent eyes superimposed over the looming white figure. The face of his son faded. His mind froze, denying its white translucent head. It sprawled over his body, the size of a bag of luggage. Wet black eyes spread in a smiling crescent with the huge outer pair casting a human visage. Its white bristled legs flexed with hairy palps buzzing around its unfolding fangs.

Blood rushed to his head, his hand slapping at one

of its legs—thick-bristled, like scuffed plastic but wet—feverish. Casey screamed and kicked as it dug in its legs, piercing him like knives. He pushed back into the corner of the bedroom where bed met wall, "JESUS CHRIST!"

It flicked the sheet off with its legs before arching its belly and flailing its legs into the air.

He scraped his ankle, planting his foot beneath the metal bed frame and overturning the mattress as he yelled.

It retreated in a flurry of spindly legs, turned almost all the way round, then turned back and bolted through the door.

Casey stood in the corner of the room, panting. "Son of a…" He ran to the hallway door and peered to the left as it darted behind a corner of the hallway. Casey went back and got the flashlight, whipping it round corners of the hallway and ceiling.

It wasn't downstairs in the family room or in the closet. He scanned the dining room and den; its legs made the card-shuffling sound. He burst through the kitchen doorway and flashed his beam over its unnaturally still body, legs folded in close; dreaming. It skittered to life with tapping claws as it spun and moved backward, toward the cellar door, flailing legs at him before slinking down the stairs. Casey ran forward, slamming the door, pulling the knob to ensure it had latched. "Damn."

He felt lightheaded as he walked upstairs to put on clothes. It had really happened; he was sure of it. He wasn't just under stress. But weird things happened. Drill Sergeant Mavers from Basic had killed himself two years ago in a hotel and nobody knew why. Maybe this was how it started. You think you see things. He looked down at the scratches on his legs and a tear in his boxers. That thing did it. It was a spider. A White-Daddy? That kid said something like that. Was there some local folklore surrounding that thing? He put on his t-shirt and jeans and shoes. He didn't know anyone in town who could help him and telling others might not be a good idea if he ever expected to sell the house.

He grabbed a shotgun and shells out of his bedroom closet. The box of shells looked like it had been wet and the paper of the .410 cartridges were a variety of dark reds. He unlatched the breach and stared down barrels with the help of the flashlight. Sergeant Mavers always shouted during rifle inspections, "Your weapon is your life, Mets! Guard your life!" He inspected the hammers and triggers before loading each barrel.

It wasn't just the scratches on his legs. There had been signs all over if he'd only put it together. Those deflated possum corpses. That's how spiders ate; they paralyzed you with their fangs, dissolved your insides and sucked you out. That hole near the back of the flue in the basement: that was where it came from. It came from the caves in those bluffs behind the house. Casey stuffed his pocket with shells, grabbed his laptop. He'd wait the thing out in the kitchen. His Gladiator DVD would keep his mind busy, even if he had to wait all night. It probably only came out at night.

He ran the DVD with the sound off and poured a coffee mug half-full with Grey Goose, wishing he had vermouth. It was all right to drink now that this had happened. The two other kitchen doors were closed so it couldn't get past. He opened the cellar door slowly, peering inside with the flashlight and the shotgun. Nothing.

The chair was hard with the drink sharp and pungent in the dirty mug and the shotgun resting over the wooden table with hammers cocked. The flashlight pointed at the black doorway and his finger rested against the trigger guard. He divided attention between the screen and the doorway, sipping vodka. He could figure this out. Figure out what he was up against. It was fast. And when he touched it, it was hot. He didn't expect spiders to be hot. But this was an enormous spider.

In his engineering classes, systems didn't always work as well when you scaled them up. Especially thermal systems. It was a surface-area to volume thing. Bigger things weren't always as thermally efficient. And spiders didn't have sweat glands or tongues to pant with to cool themselves. So maybe they'd lived in the caves before. Nobody knew how extensive and deep those caves were. Maybe they lived down there to regulate their temperatures.

He used the glow from the computer screen to read

his watch: 2:18. It was quiet outside; no crickets, no owls. The kitchen window had been broken and nailed over with particle board, letting moonlight slivers streak across his back onto the counter and cupboards to his right. The card shuffling sound came from somewhere down there.

It seemed too coincidental that he'd seen one of these things and nobody else really knew of them. Something must have changed recently. Like the farmers drained the aquifer that fed streams in their caves. Screwed up their ecosystem. Starved them out of their natural habitat. Made them come out into the heat.

On the computer, Casey watched Russell Crowe and Richard Harris discuss the future of Rome as his eyes grew heavy. He looked to the doorway. Maybe the light scared it. He turned off the flashlight and waited for his eyes to adjust. He could just see the doorframe and the floor. It was enough. He looked to the screen and whispered, "And what is Rome, Maximus?"

He checked his watch again. Thirty minutes had passed. He thought maybe he had dozed off for a minute or two so he slapped his cheek and blinked. It seemed the spider's white legs pawed the lower ledge of the doorway, but they weren't.

It had attacked him earlier. Totally unprovoked. Spiders didn't do that. Did they? Animal lovers on nature shows talked about how snakes and tarantulas were noble creatures, only attacking when provoked. But that was bullshit. Spiders were carnivores; hunters.

Every animal on this planet had developed an understanding, a suite of instincts toward every other animal, based on one thing: size. This spider didn't just pop-up on the scene overnight. It evolved over millions of years, side-by-side with humans, testing its limits, apparently, successfully since no one seemed to know of them.

It knew it was on equal footing. It would come upstairs.

He thought about how hard he had worked during the day. Now he couldn't sleep because of this. It seemed unreal. He wished he was in a nice soft hotel bed in Boston. The Hilton. A king-sized bed at the Hilton. He smiled as he eyed the black doorway.

Casey jerked his head up. Something was different. His computer screen was blurry and he couldn't see the doorway. His eyes focused on his watch: 3:40. The doorway was empty. Silence. A sensation shot through his spine as neck hairs prickled. He spun, knocking the chair, jarring the table and pointed the flashlight, clicking the switch. Nothing. He clicked it again, and again. Darkness. He tried to make out counters behind the streaks of moonlight separating the room. The clicking sound came from the far side.

He stepped backward into the cellar door, slamming it close. "Gotcha." His barrel rose as he walked toward moonlight in the center of the room.

It ran the perimeter, springing from counter to floor like a pile of deformed bones tumbling and twitching around a shell body that seemed to roll over waves.

Casey followed the card-shuffling with his barrel, spinning circles until he wasn't sure what direction it moved. The shuffling of two-clawed legs over tiles quickened. Dangling bristles flashed past in the moonlight and he spun to where it had been. It ran behind him as he spun. It came forward, curling-finger palps quivering around fangs, wet eyes glinting. The barrel rose. The hammer clicked. Misfire. It darted to the right and scurried behind him. Casey spun, head dizzy as he pictured the deflated possums on his lawn. He turned the shotgun over like a club with the tangle of white bristly legs lunging. The stock crashed onto its back, thin legs prodding and pushing him about like swords. A bang issued, his leg burning furious pain as he fell and the spider dashed and leapt onto the sink.

"It shot me!" Casey cried, crawling toward the kitchen's back door, dragging the shotgun. He staggered onto his good leg, bursting through the door.

The thing had shot him. As if it had known the second cartridge wasn't rain-soaked and had deliberately crammed its leg inside the trigger guard. He stumbled across the dining room into the family room and waited with his back against the front door, his hand warm with blood. The buckshot had grazed the outside of his right thigh. He unlatched the barrel, ejecting shells. The room spun and his pulse beat his neck. His hand dug into his pocket, shaking shells onto the floor. He clenched a shell and fumbled in the darkness to stuff it into the breach as shuffling came from the dining room, darting about chaotically.

Casey opened the front door and closed it behind him, dropping the open-breached shotgun in the grass near the Porsche. He found the magnetic key compartment under the wheel well, then climbed into the driver's seat.

"The morning. Wait till the morning." The woods seemed so still. There had to be a way to kill that thing. He wasn't sure. He couldn't force the idea out of his mind that it had shot him. It didn't matter and there was no way it could get inside the car. Still, he checked to make sure the doors were locked before resting his eyes.

He awoke to a hand tapping the windshield. The man wore a white terrycloth bathrobe. As Casey tilted his head, he noticed a white robe wrapped around his bare shoulders as well. He got out of the car and recognized Sergeant Mavers' broad strong features but the sergeant's hair was long and wet, his thick neck was flushed and beaded with water like he'd just finished a shower.

"Sergeant Mavers?" Casey looked around at the woods and the house, bewildered. "Why are we wearing Holiday Inn bathrobes?"

Mavers stared at the full silver moon and the brown and silver ridges of limestone bluffs. "Not much time left before sunrise."

Casey walked closer to Mavers but something stopped him. He felt brimming strength within Mavers.

As if he might swell up and fill the sky. "Sergeant... what happened to your hair?"

"You've got a job to finish. Don't you, Mets?" Mavers looked at him. His pupils dilated, flooding fear and wonder into the pit of Casey's stomach.

Casey flinched and steadied himself on the hood of the Porsche. His leg burned and blood from his thigh soaked through white terrycloth. "It shot me, Sergeant." His lips trembled. "It's smart." He clenched his eyes.

"This is bigger than you, Mets. You've got obligations. Did you forget, Mets? Did you think I would let you forget? Obligations: To Country. To men, Mets. That thing in your house is an abomination. It's gone against God. The God we both love!"

Casey shrunk closer to the car. "I—"

Mavers raised a clenched fist. His voice boomed like thunder, stealing into the depths of Casey's heart and lifting up on low shimmering soot clouds. "Genesis 1:26... God said, 'I made man in my image so he shall have dominion and rule over all creatures!"

His starry eyes fixed on the Sergeant, mouth gaping. "Dominion..." he said while in the Sergeant's starry-eyed trance as he pushed from the car and blinked.

Mavers went to him, his face full of fake sympathy, corners of his mouth fighting a grin. "Don't you love this country God's given us? Don't you want to be a man? Don't you deserve that house?"

Casey touched the blood of his leg and looked to dry

skin resting over a possum's ribcage. Mavers grabbed his head and turned it away. "Don't look at that!"

"It's my house," Casey said. "Not the bugs'." His head drooped to the ground. "I could get help in the morning. There could be someone in town who knows how to take care of it."

Mavers looked irritated, like his time was being wasted. "Mets. What's your best weapon? What's your best weapon, Mets?"

"My mind."

"Use it. We both know damn well this house ain't selling to anybody out of town. But that's okay. Hill-jacks got money. It spends just the same. You let word out in Shukley's there's a White-Daddy running loose on your property—you'll never sell that house."

"Gotta sell the house."

"That's right, Mets. Gotta sell it." Mavers led him to the other side of the car. He walked to the shotgun lying in the grass. "What's this?" He picked up the gun and his face flashed red. "You let your weapon get away from you?" He snapped the breach close.

"It's a hundred-years-old, Sergeant."

He held the shotgun out toward Casey. "BULL-SPIT! She's a sweet lady. She'll clean house like a Mexican."

Casey limped over, took the gun and examined it. He looked behind his shoulder to Mavers walking toward the woods. "Where you going, Sergeant?"

"We've both got things to do, Mets. It's checkout time for me but you've still got twenty minutes before sunrise and you're getting blood all over that ridiculous car you love so much."

Casey arched his neck, mumbling, "Sunrise... sunrise. Before sunrise." His eyes opened and his watch showed 4:22. His thigh didn't seem to be bleeding but it burned as he climbed out of the car.

The shotgun rested in the grass and he pulled five shells out of his pocket, holding them to the moonlight, dropping darker red casings into the grass. It was quiet outside as he hobbled and grunted up the porch stairs with the barrel bouncing in front.

The door swung inward with a creak and Casey peered inside at darkness. Listening for the scuttling, he cocked hammers and tried to make out folds in the drop cloth he knew draped over a couch in the middle of the room.

Casey crossed the threshold and pulled the door close against his back. It was dark except for rectangular grids of moonlight cast over the left side of the room by windows. He limped away from the door, listening. It was quiet. He heard his breaths and slowed them as he fanned the barrel slowly across the room. He stepped toward the center, feeling it in there. It had its white legs folded up in a ball somewhere. The air stirred. Smooth fangs scraped his shooting hand. The thing was soundless. One of the hammers fell with a click. Another misfire and he pushed his arm out, dropping the gun, pushing underneath the slick head as bristly legs beat over his face and back. Its legs shuffled and he fell to his hands and knees. Groping for the gun. Waiting for fangs in the back of his neck. His fingers found the rifle stock and the shuffling began in erratic fits and starts. He stood, limping backward just outside the light of the windows.

It grew quiet as he rested his finger on the unspent trigger. He wondered about the toxicity of its venom and felt over his shooting hand, unsure if its fangs had broken skin. His neck muscles burned. It was so quiet. It waited. He wished he could see his hand. His finger and wrist seemed tight and his heart pounded against his chest as sweat crept into his eyes. Contours and shapes were almost visible in the darkness. He pointed the barrel at them and groaned, needing to switch hands—shoot with his left before the venom cramped up his right. It was waiting. He stomped his foot. "I'm here! Right here." Shuffling within the darkness moved it closer, closer—farther, maybe.

If it paralyzed him, it could devour him slowly. Clock-like movements as it loomed. Dead inhuman eyes. His deflated corpse tugged slowly into the lawn.

The smiling crescent of eyes bounced as it rushed him and he stepped into the rectangular moonlight of window casements. He passed the shotgun to his left hand, stumbling on his right leg, falling backward, finger squeezing along the unspent trigger.

It turned sideways, running along the wall as Casey kicked backward into the corner and propped the gun over his knee. White legs pattered along window panes like a gale of raindrops. Casey followed the welded BB at the end of the barrel as it wobbled toward the white flurry, pulling the trigger with the muzzle flashing red as the stock kicked into his bicep. Buckshot punched a tennis-ball-sized hole where the head fused with the thorax. Its right legs collapsed, bringing it to the floor as legs kicked and bounced it randomly, clear fluid spewing, flapping chunks of white shell around the hole.

Palps buzzed and motionless eyes glared as it dragged toward him with one front leg while the rest went berserk like discordant arms. They stopped suddenly while the last leg pulled closer, staring. Casey brought his heel down on the leg, cracking and bursting its hot fluid, seeping through jeans and sock. He looked into its huge wet eyes. Inside its simple mind, it still crawled toward him. It had won somewhere deep inside there.

He laughed forcefully, rolling his head between windowpanes and feeding eyes, laughing until his throat hurt and tears rolled over his cheeks.

His palms pressed over the walls as he stood, then he kicked the carcass along the floor. It was heavy. He considered jumping with both feet onto the soft hairy abdomen and bursting it but he didn't want the memory of what it would feel and sound like burned into his brain. Casey opened the front door and kicked it several times, bouncing its lifeless legs before getting it over the threshold and onto the porch. "Get out, bug!"

He inspected his right hand in the moonlight. The

fangs hadn't broken skin, only scratched the surface in a red streak.

Casey was surprised to find himself tired. He had to get a few things set right before trying for a couple hours sleep. Like closing that cellar door, reloading his shotgun, inspecting the wound in his leg; he'd at least need to put some iodine on it, eventually. He pulled the curtain off and took a short watchful shower.

The bedroom door closed behind him. He slept on his side, facing the door with the shotgun. Casey closed his eyes and thought about throwing cement in the hole in the basement. Then he could finish the repairs and get the hell out of Shuckley's. With some white paint, new carpet, a new toilet, he could show the house to a real-estate agent. But a notion occurred to him that seemed half-inspired by stubborn pride. The house had a certain feel to it that he was beginning to like. Maybe he wouldn't sell it after all. Maybe he needed to slow down for a while and enjoy the country. Hell, it was his house after all; not the bugs'

THE NATURAL CELEBRITY

ROY WASN'T A big guy. That was the mystery of it. How could something so big come out of a 145 pound guy with a black crew-cut and skinny bird-like hands? Sure, in the duration of his thirty-four years, he'd looked into the stool from time to time, thinking, "Hey? that's really big," but he never thought it could take him anywhere. He'd grown to accept his mediocrity, his failures. I mean, after the divorce, being fired from dry-walling and the dishonorable discharge from the army for insubordination, he understood he was the guy that worked the telemarketing job, the one that wanted to leave the mobile homes but would die in them like his father had, regardless.

Until his friend sent him an email. It had a link to a listing of websites of the world's strangest competitions and there were thousands. How could that be, right? Thousands. But there were the kind-of weird ones: grape-eating, professional videogame playing, and the sadistic ones: finger-cutting, lifting stuff with parts of your body, and the supernatural ones: mind reading, vampire dueling. Towards the bottom, something caught Roy's eye: 14th Annual International Stooley Tournament. It was hard for Roy to believe at first: an international competition with prize money in the hundreds of thousands where the winner only had to have a stool outweighing all others? Roy's first thought was there was finally and definitely much too many people on this world. His second thought was maybe... just maybe. He found an eight-hundred number at the bottom of the Stooley webpage and dialed.

A grizzled old hag answered. "Hello, International Stooley Registration."

"Yah... in the competition, you just measure how big they is?"

"We measure the competitor's stool-weight in ounces. Heftiest wins. It's that simple buck-o."

"I makes 'em big."

"How big?" she inquired, dubiously.

"You'll see." And he hung up the phone right there, merely providing the courtesy of letting them know he was coming.

The single elimination tournament was a grueling fourteen-day undertaking. Each day an Offering was made to the twenty-person judging panel and the ranks of the original four-hundred competitors were thinned considerably. The amount of people that came to see the competition seemed a little strange at first. But people had always worshiped each other for strange reasons, reasons that got stranger all the time. Reality TV celebrities by the dozens, vapid runway models, heiresses and socialites: they all had the ear of the press and the public.

It was all a little intense for most, but not Roy. He'd always eaten as much as he could. Food hated him, refused to stay with him, like oil and water. But he loved food and it was all free. He first met Dr. Vickers in the contestant's cafeteria. The Doctor sat by himself as usual.

"Anyone sitting here, mister?" Roy asked.

"Clearly there isn't. And it's doctor."

Roy sat. "What you a doctor in?"

The doctor stopped worrying and masticating a barbeque chicken leg and slapped his hand to a thin aluminum box about the size of a TV remote with buttons. He eyed Roy suspiciously, "Quantum Mechanics. You won't steal my invention!"

"What's a Quantum for?"

"Oh, you know. Possibilities. Maybe an electron's here, maybe it's over there. Maybe your brain is normal and healthy like the rest of us or maybe, perhaps my boy, it's full of marmalade, about to burst, owing to the pressure."

"Hey, jerk. I just wanted to talk to you. Ain't my fault you some freak that sits by hisself every damn day."

"You won't defeat me, boy. I've watched you advancing through the rounds, watched you like a spider that spins his web and waits. I've won the Stooley seven years in a row. And you won't stand between my rightful place in history. You haven't the stomach nor the girth. It's a sport of kings, you see, and I'm sorry."

*

In the finals Roy was pitted against Dr. Vickers. Both competitors were assigned opposing blue stalls within the amphitheater. Dr. Vickers had emerged a half-hour earlier, weighing in at a confident 565 ounces—a world record. He relaxed in the waiting room, getting a neck massage, posturing, chatting-up reporters. But his eyes flicked occasionally to the TV screen with its image of Roy's sweat-beaded forehead and that look in his eyes like Roy was going somewhere—somewhere—yes—perhaps never returning.

But Roy emerged from the booth two hours later, pale and disheveled. Vickers pushed his huge bulk through loiterers and spectators back toward the stage. Cameras zoomed in on Roy's floating birth, projecting it to the huge panoramic grid of screens for the capacity crowd's eager inspection.

"We're getting the weight," the announcer said. "Hold on. It's coming. 569. 569!"

The crowd cheered. Vickers stopped and hung his head.

"We have ourselves a new International Champion!" the announcer said.

"Hold on," another announcer said. "Zoom in on it. Zoom in, damnit. Zoom! There. There! It's—it's Abe

Lincoln. You see. That top hat. That chin, the eyes. The eyes, man! My God! It's him... It's him."

"My God!"

That alone wouldn't have been enough. No. There was a predestined culmination. Roy stood, tired, swaying, head swimming, he said into his microphone, scanning the oceanic crowd of hushed faces, with such deadpan, such poise, "For score—seven plops ago." The crowd blazed laughter. And a new star blazed there on that stage. The commissioner rushed the stage and extended with straining arms the Stooley to him. Both men raised the platinum sculpture of a man perched atop a toilet with sculpted chin resting in a tiny hand's palm—a look of stoic grace in the statue's chiseled silver features.

Roy knew then he had something. Not a gift or calling but a talent. And it was more than he'd ever asked. No one could take his talent from him. But that didn't stop some scientists from trying. They claimed the 569-ouncer was impossible for a man his size. They said he had to of brought matter with him into the stall, kept it warm in a tube strapped to his leg—long-legging they called it. These allegations were, of course... bullshit.

The public adored him. He didn't train, he didn't strive or yearn. He wasn't in-shape or intelligent or passionate. But he was exceptional. The fact couldn't be contested. He was pure and he was simple. He dropped his pants and did what he was born to do. It was abundantly clear for the first time in history that absolutely anybody could have it all and for no apparent reason. Kids looked up to Roy. Standardized test scores dropped. Parents encouraged their kids to eat like Roy. Graduation rates faltered.

And the endorsements rolled in for Roy. But Roy refused to change his diet, to eat what the science of the sport prescribed. With the fiber-switching and the starches, the purge/binge cycles. He let the companies of the foods he already ate sponsor him. With checks rolling in he could afford to move out of the mobile homes. But he'd grown comfortable. So he bought-out all the residents and had the modules connected in a chain. A coiling chain that from aerial view some said looked just like, well, you know.

Dr. Vickers dropped out of the competitor's circuit after his defeat and Roy won the Stooley year-after-year. So much so that some wondered if he should even bother to let the platinum statue leave his palace of coiling mobile units.

Roy worked his way into the mainstream of pop culture a little at a time. Television discussion panels invited him on for the simple comedic juxtaposition of him sitting amidst veteran journalists and political pundits. While discussing the nuclear proliferation of Second-World countries within the context of an unregulated information age, Roy chimed in, "Reckon if President just close his eyes and sticks to his business, everything comes out fine." The tone of discussion never recovered.

The show was cancelled to make room for one about torturing friends for money.

Roy looked back over his seven-year career and realized he had amassed considerable wealth. He had sufficient funds so that he could sail himself, his entourage and his band of well-wishers comfortably through retirement. This would be his final International Stooley Tournament. Win or lose he would pass the Stooley on to the next generation of feasting competitors. In the weeks prior to the competition, he went about his business fairly calmly, confident in his decision, when the telephone rang.

"Hello," Roy said.

"I made one bigger than you this morning."

Roy cringed. "Who this is?"

"I made one bigger than you this morning, as I have every morning. You fool, did you think the spider had stopped spinning his web." The phone clicked. Roy thought to check his caller ID, but he knew who it was. Dr. Vickers had come out of retirement for one last fight.

Roy paid a member of his entourage to pose as a journalist. The false journalist hid among a cluster of reporters waiting outside the amphitheatre during the commencement ceremony. When Dr. Vickers arrived in his limousine and walked up the red carpet, this spy pushed past the others to ask, "Dr. Vickers! Dr. Vickers! Is it true you came out of retirement for the soul purpose of exacting revenge on Roy?"

Vickers brushed his way through the bustling reporters undaunted.

"Dr. Vickers!"

"My dear lad, I don't get caught up in the politics. I
came here to poop."

The spy reported back to Roy. Roy glanced up in
a daze before hurling his champagne flute against the
wall and pulling his ruby embroidered bathrobe close.
"Damnit!" The pedicurist looked down. "That Doctor's
up to something! He never believed it were real. He
never believed in Honest-Abe." He rubbed his hands
over his temples, "I—I just can't think." Well-wishers
encircled with back-patting and flattery.

But at the competition, the Doctor was eliminated
in the third round. Still Roy was not appeased. He had
his people try to follow Vickers but it was as if he had
vanished.

Roy advanced through the tournament as expected—
virtually uncontested. In the finals he sat in his stall
beside an Italian opponent of greatly inferior skill.

"Well," the announcer began, "Do you think we'll
see another Honest-Abe out of Roy tonight."

"No. I fear we'll never witness sportsmanship of that
caliber again. You know... wait a second. What's happening with Roy?"

"That's the look. He gets it right before he wins each
Stooley."

"No. It's something else."

A woman in the crowd stood and screamed, "He's dying!"

Roy's face twitched. He groaned and slumped over before the final plop. A plop echoing over loudspeakers through the silent amphitheater that faded to the sound of Dr. Vickers as he clapped slowly, walking up the empty center aisle. Vickers reached the stage and snatched an idle hand microphone. "Good evening," he addressed the mute crowd. "I say again, good evening. Has it been so long, my friends, that you don't recognize your own, Dr. Vickers? Very well, your beloved Roy has died of aneurism. A failing common to the profession. We can add a lack of staying power to his list of crimes, the greatest of which being the forgery of his talents. Roy never birthed Honest-Abe. This is a matter of fact. And this other remaining competitor isn't a shadow of what I was in my prime." He scanned over the crowd.

The sound rose up slowly from somewhere in the nosebleed seats, like a soft thrumming, "Roy. Roy. Roy," growing—reaching its way to the stage.

"And yet you loved him. Despite his false prowess. You stupid, stupid lemmings. No man that size could make something like that."

"ROY! ROY! ROY! ROY!"

Security guards in gray shirts encircled the stage, encroaching on the doctor.

"Ah, but wait!" the doctor's eyes flashed bravado, "Wait and see what, with your blessing, I propose." The doctor stepped toward the center table where the platinum statue rested. His eyes grew. "Simply give me back my prize. And all—all is forgiven." Guards rushed him, restrained him as his open hands strained toward the stoic face of the gleaming man atop his stool.

"ROY! ROY! ROY!" The crowd stood, pumping arms to the ceiling.

The doctor lurched forward and a guard strangled around his thigh. "Roy, you... you long-legging, impos-ter-ing son-of-a-bitch."

An elderly woman in the front rows jeered him. He retorted, "You wouldn't know talent if it sat on your own stool!"

NOVEL SAMPLE:

GROWING UP WIRED
by
David Wallace Fleming

A S A DIVERSION, I followed the Can Man around campus—always from a safe distance because he was shy. Was he John the Baptist incarnate? It was too soon to know, though he wore a waist-long, unkempt gray beard with black striations and the bees loved him, buzzing near, hovering for the sugary remnants on his tan arthritic fingers and those gooey flecks inside the cans of the clear garbage sack slung over his shoulder.

He listlessly pedaled his forest-green, 1970s ten-speed over sidewalks and jarringly wobbled up a curb with a "shit-SHIT!" bursting as if a lethal sneeze. He rambled, to himself and perhaps unseen past enemies, friends, lovers—of song remnants married to dimming emotions—the dueling nonsense maxims of God and Satan. His desert might have been one of loneliness among tight-skinned twenty-one-year-olds with his crumbly, green flip flops serving as thong sandals and dime-store, twelve-year-old clothes his camel-hair robe.

It's unclear why I followed the Can Man. I had presumed him alcoholic and schizophrenic. I imagined him pressed flat against the lowest strata, the weight of our riches and comfort pinning him fast as the water in a lightless ocean trench crushes a man from the vertical miles resting above.

Hindsight is 20/20. It seems obvious with the passage of years that I followed the Can Man because I believed him alcoholic and with three men on my father's side suffering from this I needed to know this Can Man was a different species from what I was, that a twitch of destiny could never shove me in his place.

He came early in the mornings around seven-thirty, so I had to set my alarm to catch him. It was still a week before the start of the fall semester. The prior evening I had drunk beer on the patio and I was hung-over as I dressed and slipped on shower sandals. I sat on a wooden bench next to a stone tablet of our fraternal crest. The patio was scattered with aluminum cans and glass beer bottles. There were maybe fifty of them. The Can Man would come.

He was a creeper, that Can Man. Like a house fly on your arm before you knew it. I startled as I looked up from my daydreaming to him picking up the cans set along the long wooden bench like parapets. He worked solemnly, though he mumbled, "Devil" with each crumpled can he threw in his clear sack and "Saint-ey", lisping childishly as he poured stale beer out of full ones. "Devil, Devil, Saint-ey," his gaunt face froze and then tilted on his thin neck, fingers infrequently tugging at ring-tabs and sliding over aluminum as a blind man reads brail.

"Hey, Can Man," I exclaimed.

He looked up—right at me, but without malice, setting a can down before picking up his bike to sneak away. He did this with such fluidity, such a smooth and eloquent escape that I wasn't able to protest. The alcohol left undigested after my sleep had made me bold yet too dumb to get him to stay. It was a week before we had enough drinking guests over to warrant another Can Man visit.

This morning there were only twenty or so cans and bottles. So I went downstairs to a room we called the Pit-Pit because it was vaguely connected to the Pit through the TV room. This was where the pledges stored their cans and bottles that they would use to fund a charter bus trip to visit another fraternity at some other campus of their choice. I went down there to steal a bag full of cans and bottles. It was a heavy, rattling bag. It would draw in the Can Man. As I neared the stairwell I met a pledge, the pledge-class president, no less.

"Hey!" he said. "What do you think you're doing with our cans?"

"They're not just your cans," I said. "I bought some of these cans."

"You can't do that. If you take them, I'm going to tell Rex." (Our fraternal president).

I set the bag down. "Look. I need these." I looked up at the ceiling tiles and reached into my wallet. "I'll just pay for them." I handed him a twenty, hating myself because all I had on me were two twenties.

"I retract my former statement." He picked up his basket and continued on to the laundry room.

The extra cans and bottles were scattered around the porch quickly so no one saw and in random places to look natural. I waited on the bench. His bicycle made a slight squeak that I had trained my ears to hear. When I heard his I looked down at the red bricks, trying to be inconspicuous as he considered whether to begin collecting. Cans rattled and rustled into his plastic sack as I looked down. "Saint-ey." Beer poured and his footsteps paced bricks, "Devil. Devil."

I stood. "Excuse me, sir." I walked toward him.

He looked up, heading toward his bike. "I don't want your cans."

"No, please. I'd like to talk with you."

His hand motioned to push me away. "Proper channels. Proper channels," he said.

"What? What proper channels?" I asked, nearing him.

"Call your governor. We'll have a man out in twelve minutes or it's free?"

"What's free?" I asked.

He looked around, upset. "Everything! Everything,

man, don't you know that? It's free." He spoke loud with a lisping apostle's rage. He looked up to the sky. Then raised a crushed beer can and showed the decay in his smile, "Why do you throw it away?"

"I don't know," I said. "Actually, I'd like very much for you to have these cans."

The Can Man picked a can off the ground. "I've been picking up for you kids for one hundred years." He looked up at me. "It's time. Go into the world. Get a job!"

I followed at a distance as he walked to a carnation planter with beer cans covering its oak rim. He stooped down before the planter and picked a can crushed into a disk off the red bricks. "You see that? That's a Big Nic. Nickel got too big. Carry her back to my spot; flip her for a nickel that spends." He scrounged over the cans on the rim. "Devil, Devil," he poured beer, "Some Saint-ey in this here."

As a breeze moved past him, green horse manure and burning leaves flashed to mind with the fear of confronting someone so dazed and inhuman settling in my throat. "Where do you sleep?" I asked.

"World."

"What?" I asked.

He didn't look up. "World. I sleep at the world, the outside part."

"Oh." I scratched my head. "Where was that again?"

"Under rocks. Specs of sand—inside them; I do. The sleepy brains of strong-fisted police marble-ers. Up the butt of that beagle. And the crawlspace of public librar-ies. Sometimes I sleep also, there."

"What are you doing to prepare for the future?"

"Future?" he asked.

"It's what happens next."

"Ah. No. I, I don't think so," his voice wavered and softened, "It don't happen next."

"Well, actually it does. Like earlier we talked about something and now we're talking about something dif-ferent. Time passed between that. Take that and extend it out to a really large scale. That's the future."

"Scale? You going to punch? I hit first, last." He pointed to his thumbnail's old, dry wound cleaved to the cuticle. "I hit you in between."

"I'm saying that time passes and things happen. We have to prepare for what's to come. You know? winter's coming and it's going to get cold. Don't you remember things that happened to you when you were young?"

"Sure! Sure, man: things." His eyes lit and moved like a child with so many presents. "They happen, they always happen. Bling blang bloom, they come at you and they move out like, like... Things are always hap-pening. It don't stop, it don't start. It just is. Here we are, man. Here we are."

"But things happen, things change, one after the other, we have these events that change us like a, like a bead of paint running down a wall that can never run upward again."

"That what you think?" He patted my back with dry,

rough fingers pressing. "Sorry, man. That's a shit way to get these sidewalks and white walls figured. Keep working it. You got money, man. I don't talk shop because I like you. Need fuel to burn me up. Starting to be stuck on the tight fingers and belly."

I reached into my pocket and pulled out a bill. It was a twenty—all I had. He saw it. A twenty wasn't something to be easily parted with. I had less than three-thousand in checking. Boozing and maintaining an early nineties domestic car, such as the Plymouth Laser, didn't come cheap.

"Here," I said.

He stuffed it into the pocket of his cargo shorts, wordlessly. The shorts didn't suit him. Both he and the manufacturer had spent time fatiguing.

"Where were you born," I asked. "Do you have relatives?"

He looked around like someone was watching, then headed to a black barbeque grill made of a halved barrel with angle-iron legs. He collected the cans around its legs. "Devil, Devil. Big Nic!" He toppled a Corona bottle to pour its yellow beer. "Mom and Dad were gone. Grandma was a waitress. Ink-black hair with length and eyes for sex-crash; then her face fell to the floor; bones shrunk." He walked toward the couch beneath the roof's overhang, throwing cans in his bag. "Devil. Devil. Hmm." He ran a swollen-knuckled finger along his oily face and neck. "I stepped on a nail in the alleys when I was five-years. We couldn't afford the shot to keep away trap-jaw. Trappity-trap. Trappity." He shook his bag of cans and looked through it.

"Did you just wait and see if you would be okay?"

"We went to the guy, the busy guy—slicing, hacking—big slow... fingers! pinky finger not here on this one or there on that one—he was pulling babies out of a screamy—well—the too-old, the too-young whores in a lost freezer of Restaurant." The Can Man placed the last can inside the weighty bag and slung it over his back. "We're done here." He squinted at the sun. "Ain't no heaven, but I ain't afraid to be dead. I seen enough for it to be enough."

Growing up Wired is available on Amazon.com

ABOUT THE AUTHOR

DAVID WRITES A little of everything, but mostly satire and humor. He's been writing fiction for practically his entire life. He writes the kind of stories that he'd like to see written and wants to give readers something special and reflective of the exciting times in which we live.

His short stories have appeared in Out of the Gutter, Escape Velocity and the Bizarro Press. Check out his poems at davidwallacefleming.com

www.ingramcontent.com/pod-product-compliance
Lightning Source LLC
Chambersburg PA
CBHW021038130626
46552CB00005B/1911